Sexual Solidarity

"Gay Ex-Mormons Unite!" In these tales by a former Mormon missionary, a polygamist in 1855 Utah is ordered to take a fourth wife, when all he really wants is to be with another man. A Victorian enthusiast has a startling sexual revelation to make at his monthly Society meeting. A gay Mormon hires a hit man in a desperate bid to stop himself from breaking the Law of Chastity.

A Relief Society president is trapped on a plane next to a gay man flaunting his sexuality. The Three Nephites seek counseling to deal with their sexual frustrations since their wives aren't immortal as they are. A worthy gay man becomes a ministering angel in the afterlife. A Mormon missionary in Italy moves in with a man he's been teaching.

Gay men don't always have lots in common, but most of us understand religious bigotry and enjoy reading some of the many ways we've learned not only to cope but also find *"Sexual Solidarity"* with one another.

Praise for Johnny Townsend

In *Zombies for Jesus*, "Townsend isn't writing satire, but deeply emotional and revealing portraits of people who are, with a few exceptions, quite lovable."

Kel Munger, *Sacramento News and Review*

In *Sex among the Saints,* "Townsend writes with a deadpan wit and a supple, realistic prose that's full of psychological empathy….he takes his protagonists' moral struggles seriously and invests them with real emotional resonance."

Kirkus Reviews

Inferno in the French Quarter: The UpStairs Lounge Fire is "a gripping account of all the horrors that transpired that night, as well as a respectful remembrance of the victims."

Terry Firma, Patheos

"Johnny Townsend's 'Partying with St. Roch' [in the anthology *Latter-Gay Saints*] tells a beautiful, haunting tale."

Kent Brintnall, Out in Print: Queer Book Reviews

Selling the City of Enoch is "sharply intelligent…pleasingly complex…The stories are full of…doubters, but there's no vindictiveness in these pages; the characters continuously poke holes in Mormonism's more extravagant absurdities, but they take very little pleasure in doing so….Many of Townsend's stories…have a provocative edge to them, but this [book] displays a great deal of insight as well…a playful, biting and surprisingly warm collection."

Kirkus Reviews

Gayrabian Nights is "an allegorical tour de force…a hard-core emotional punch."

Gay. Guy. Reading and Friends

The Washing of Brains has "A lovely writing style, and each story [is] full of unique, engaging characters….immensely entertaining."

Rainbow Awards

In *Dead Mankind Walking*, "Townsend writes in an energetic prose that balances crankiness and humor….A rambunctious volume of short, well-crafted essays…"

Kirkus Reviews

Johnny Townsend

Sexual Solidarity

Johnny Townsend

Print ISBN: 979-8-9883389-4-9
Ebook ISBN: 979-8-9883389-5-6

[Selected stories from *The Mormon Victorian Society*, *Despots of Deseret*, *Dragons of the Book of Mormon*, and *Mormon Fairy Tales*.]

Printed on acid-free paper.

2023

First Edition

Cover design by BetiBup33 Studio Design

Contents

The Mormon Victorian Society

Ben wondered what he could do for Show and Tell tonight. The members of the Mormon Victorian Society here in Salt Lake met on the third Thursday of each month at a different member's home. Most of the members lived in the Avenues in homes constructed during the Victorian era. Some lived as far away as Sugar House. Another member lived right across the street from the LDS Conference Center, a stone's throw from Temple Square.

While it was undeniable that the Conference Center was a lovely building, the Society members preferred buildings that had been constructed, of course, during the Victorian period. They sometimes had outings to the Salt Lake temple, to gaze at its breathtaking craftsmanship, and they occasionally went to Logan and Manti as well, and once even down to see the St. George temple.

As much as they all believed in and supported the living Church, there was no denying that temples today simply weren't as inspiring as those of the late 1800's.

Some people put DVDs showing a log burning in a fireplace on their TV to watch during cold winter days, just had it on in the background while they went about their day. Ben had made a mix DVD of film snippets showing his favorite street scenes from movies set in Victorian times, all either in color originally or colorized. There was no dialogue, just a soundtrack of Victorian-era music.

He played the DVD on a flatscreen he hung on his wall surrounded by a window frame, so that it felt like he was looking out the window at the Victorian city around him.

Ben flipped through the pictures in his book *Victorian Ceramic Tiles.* He'd brought the book to Show and Tell several months ago but naturally hadn't been able to turn to every single page during the few brief moments he was in front of the group. Some people brought actual Majolica tiles, others brought beautifully decorated books created during the late Victorian era, with gilded covers and gilded pages. *Queenly Women Crowned and Uncrowned* was one.

Another which had made an impression on Ben was a rather Catholic volume with the title *Fabiola.* Other people brought artwork from the period or photos of buildings constructed back in the nineteenth century. Ben had seen the Royal Albert Hall, the Victoria Law Courts in Birmingham, the Banff Springs Hotel in Alberta, and even the Painted Ladies in San Francisco.

It wasn't important that the item originate from the Salt Lake Valley, only that in some way, focusing on this period helped the Society members remember that Mormons back then had lived their values much more strongly than they did today.

Many in the group were annoyed that neighborhoods like the Avenues seemed to attract so many liberals, jack Mormons and non-Mormons. Ben wondered if that somehow made the members of the Mormon Victorian Society feel besieged, pushing them to withdraw even more from modern society.

He sometimes wondered if that was what the leaders of the Church were doing, too.

As Ben sat with the book of tile photographs on his lap, his cell phone rang. "Hello," he said, flipping the lid. Even his newfangled cell phone was old-fashioned.

"Ben, it's Mason."

Mason always wore a pocket watch. Whenever a conversation stalled, he'd pull it out and say, "It's time for you to say something" or "It's time for me to leave" or "It's time for a good time" and turn on the radio, even if it was to a contemporary pop station.

"How are you?" Ben asked him.

"Frantic about tonight. I don't have a clue what to bring."

"You have that beautiful book of Milton's poems," Ben suggested.

"Yes, but Milton isn't Victorian."

"The book is, Mason. That's what counts. It's beautiful. Books today are produced so cheaply. Books back then were meant to last."

"I don't know."

"What color are the pages?" Ben pressed.

"White, of course."

"'Of course,'" Ben mimicked. "Because they're acid-free."

"All right, I'll bring it. What about you?"

Ben sighed heavily. "I don't know yet, either."

Mason laughed. "*I* know what you should show."

"Don't even go there," Ben warned.

"Shall I pick you up at 6:45?"

"Thanks. I'll figure out something before then." Ben heard Mason's pocket watch snapping shut and closed the lid to his phone. He stared at his book again.

He liked the format for the group's meetings overall. Besides the quarterly Show and Tell sessions, there were quarterly Book Club meetings and quarterly Film Nights. For book club, they'd read Victorian books such as *Ben-Hur*, *The Prince and the Pauper*, *Treasure Island*, *King Solomon's Mines*, and *Kidnapped.* Anything written during the period that wasn't too depressing.

Whenever a Society member suggested they read Thomas Hardy, Mason would pull out his watch. "It's time to read some Raffles."

Of course, most of Hornung's stories were written after Queen Victoria died, so there weren't many they could slip past the screening committee.

The most daring they'd gotten so far was reading *The Tenant of Wildfell Hall.* It was such a relief to read stories that weren't filled with vulgarity. Even when a character cursed in these books, it was written as, "He cursed." Ben didn't have to actually see the offensive words.

The same was pretty much true of the Victorian films they watched. Lots of the Sherlock Holmes movies starring

Basil Rathbone, of course, plus *Heidi* and *The Picture of Dorian Gray* and Gilbert and Sullivan operettas such as *The Mikado* and *The Pirates of Penzance*. They cheated once and watched *The Secret Garden*, though technically that was an Edwardian piece.

They'd also tried the original *True Grit* another time, but even though it was set right in the heart of the Victorian era, the group decided that Westerns didn't count, and they stuck to urban films after that.

Ben slid his book about tiles back onto the shelf and pulled out another volume. *The Art of Publishers' Bookbindings 1815-1915.* Lots of beautiful book covers to show from those pages. Ben sat down with the book and flipped slowly through the pages. Some of the other members had joked that Ben wasn't an authentic Victorian. He didn't own anything *made* then; he always simply brought in pictures.

He did have one authentic object, of course, and that was what Mason had been referring to earlier. Ben's mother had slipped it around his penis every night as he was growing up, a tiny ring with spikes pointing inward. At the beginning of the night, the ring would just rest innocently around his penis, but if for any reason Ben began to develop an erection during the night, the spikes would dig into his growing penis, and the pain would force the erection to disappear.

The ring had been handed down from great-grandmother to grandmother to mother. Ben's mother had wanted to pass it on to her daughter after Ben left for his mission, but Ben had secreted the ring with him to England for the two years he spent there, feeling he'd need the help more than ever during this period when he wanted to be especially spiritual.

He'd continued to wear the ring for another two years after he returned to Salt Lake. It was almost like the Mormon undergarments he wore, with their fabric going down to his knees, and the sacred symbols embroidered over the knee, the navel, and the breasts.

These things reminded Ben to remain virtuous. Here he was, a relatively good-looking young man of twenty-six, and still a virgin. That ring had helped as much as Church teachings had. When Ben had confided its history to Mason just over a year ago, Mason had laughed and said, "Sheesh, you're so Puritanical."

"No, I'm not," Ben had protested. "I'm Victorian."

Mason had then gone online and searched for "Victorian" and "Salt Lake" and discovered the Mormon Victorian Society. He'd taken Ben there as a joke the first time, but to their surprise, they both found they enjoyed the meeting, and they'd been going back ever since.

Whenever they were out together and saw a man with purple hair or a woman with a tattoo of a spider on her cheek, Mason would pull out his pocket watch. "Time to plan for our next Victorian Society meeting."

Ben rather liked blue hair.

And he'd accidentally come upon a porn magazine lying on the sidewalk one day and seen a photo of a dragon tattooed on a man's penis. That wasn't so bad, either.

But he'd pulled out his flip phone immediately and called Mason. He needed his friend's moral strength.

Ben and Mason were the only two members of the Society who didn't own Victorian houses. They both still lived in apartments, but Ben had since moved to an apartment in an old Victorian place and was trying to talk Mason into moving in with him. Mason still lived in a building constructed during the 1960's. One didn't have to love Victorian architecture to hate 1960's building styles. But Mason kept resisting.

Perhaps he understood Ben's real motive.

Ben had fallen in love with Mason not long after they met at a leadership meeting. They were in the same Singles ward, serving as first and second counselor in the Elders Quorum. Mason always had lots of girls after him at the Singles dances, and Ben could understand why.

While Ben had boring, mousy brown hair, Mason had deep, rich, dark hair, almost black. Ben's hair was straight and lifeless, yet Mason's was wavy with a little curl right in front. Ben wore average, conservative clothes. Mason always wore the latest fashion. Ben was an accountant just starting out. Mason, with his MBA, was already well on his way to becoming a successful businessman. He'd have his own Victorian in the Avenues long before Ben.

But Ben knew Mason's secret. Mason was gay, too. Ben had watched as Mason's eyes had followed the other good-looking men at the dances, and sometimes even in Priesthood meeting. Ben had listened as Mason praised the good looks of both Benedict Cumberbatch and Martin Freeman in the

BBC's new version of *Sherlock Holmes*, a show not suitable for the Society but still fun for Ben and Mason to watch together on Sunday nights.

The most telling clue, though, had come when Mason insisted on seeing Ben slip on the spiked ring in front of him one night. Ben had gotten an erection just from watching Mason's riveted expression. It had hurt, of course, but the pain was certainly worth it when he saw a growing bulge in Mason's pants as well. They'd never discussed the incident since that night a year ago.

If only…

The doorbell rang right at 6:45. Mason was nothing if not punctual. Ben pulled him inside and gave him a hug. Handshakes were the norm for Mormon men, but Ben had made a bold move six months earlier and hugged Mason upon greeting him, and Mason had allowed it, so it had become their standard greeting ever since. In private, of course. They still shook hands at church.

"Have you made a decision?" Mason asked, looking around.

Ben shrugged. "Just a picture of a book. You'll have to let me go first. I can't compete with the real thing."

"But you *are* the real thing." Mason laughed.

Ben looked at him carefully to try to gauge whether it was just a joke or something more. "You are, too," he replied calmly.

Mason's smile faded for just a second, but then he plastered on a brighter one. "I still think you should show everyone your spiked ring. You don't have to tell the group you used to wear it. I think they'd get a kick out of it."

Ben shook his head. "We're going to Carol's house tonight. She even covers the legs on her piano with cloth because it's immodest for any 'leg' to be showing."

Mason rolled his eyes. "Some of the group really are a bit fanatical, aren't they?"

"The Victorian era is a difficult one for Mormons sexually." Ben watched again as Mason began to look uncomfortable. "Everything so prim and proper, and yet for us, it was also the height of our polygamy."

"Well, no one in the group is proposing we start *that* again."

"We don't really have a Lecture Night with the Society," Ben went on, "but there are lots of topics I'd enjoy hearing about. I wonder if we can get a guest lecturer to lead an informal discussion some evening in place of Movie Night or Book Club."

"I don't know. The group likes its structure."

Ben nodded, grabbed his book, and they headed out to the car. Mason drove the short distance to Carol's house. The street was already crowded. A good twenty to thirty people usually showed up each month at these events. Claire and Holly were the first of the regulars Ben saw.

The women had confided to the group several months earlier that they altered their Mormon undergarments, lengthening the sleeves to reach the wrists and the legs to reach the ankles, the way the sacred garments were worn back in the Victorian era. The rest of the group supported their decision, but Ben noticed that during the past couple of warm months, everyone except these two women always wore short sleeves.

Tonight, the third Thursday of June, both Claire and Holly looked overheated, even in the air conditioning. Their outer clothes weren't Victorian, though. No one in the group wanted to look like freaks. "This weekend's the parade," Calder said, another accountant who Ben liked. "Anyone going?"

"The Days of '47?" Carol asked. "Is it time for that already?" She offered Ben, Mason, and Calder a tray of hors d'oeuvres. The Days of '47 Parade which commemorated the Saints' arrival in Salt Lake took place near the end of July.

"Gay Pride, silly." Calder took half a sweet mini bell pepper stuffed with shredded chicken.

Ben looked nervously at Mason, who was staring very closely at his own mini bell pepper.

"Oh, do we have to talk about such unpleasant things?" Carol fingered her collar.

"There's a contingent of active Mormons marching this year. Mormons for Marriage Equality," Calder went on.

"Abominable," Carol muttered. "Back in the good old days…"

"You mean, when Oscar Wilde was writing *The Importance of Being Earnest*?" Calder smiled.

"You're horrible," said Carol, but she was smiling, too.

"Back then, they knew how to put people like that in prison," Holly said in her long sleeves. "You're new to the group, Calder. This is only your second meeting. If you want to fit in, you'll learn there are some topics best left undiscussed."

"Just like everywhere else in church." Calder sighed. "There's always an elephant in the living room."

"I'm just saying…"

"You're just *not* saying…"

"You know," Ben said boldly, his heart beating a little more rapidly than usual, "there were a lot of people in the Victorian era who had nipple rings. Even the women."

There was dead silence in the group that had gathered around Carol and Calder. Mason looked mortified. Even Calder's eyes widened a little in curious surprise.

"People have always been sexual, even when public rules were very strict," Ben continued. "There would've been no prostitutes for Jack the Ripper to kill if there hadn't been lots of prostitutes."

"Oh, good grief," Carol said. "You aren't trying to ruin the one special night we have each month, are you?"

Mason pulled out his pocket watch. "It's time to sit down." Mason grabbed Ben's arm and led him to the padded piano bench, where they sat next to each other. "Oh, my heck," he whispered to Ben. "What was that all about?"

Ben knew Mason was intrigued by piercings. Mason had let it slip one night when he and Ben were out walking downtown and passed a man with a labret. As it turned out, Ben had also always felt a little thrilled when he saw a shirtless man in the park with a nipple ring.

Of course, any shirtless man in reasonable shape would have titillated him, nipple ring or not. But after he joined the Society, he'd done some research and learned there was even a small museum in London which celebrated this little-known aspect of Victorian society. It was another time he wished there were a Lecture Night among the other activities.

Ben shrugged. "It's just that sometimes I feel people are participating in this Society to help them repress things they don't want to deal with."

"You can't *like* all the crime and sex and drugs that are a part of modern culture," Mason insisted.

"Sherlock Holmes was an opium addict."

"He wasn't a real person," Mason pointed out.

"Victorian opium dens were real."

Mason breathed out in frustration. "Young couples had chaperones then. It was a more genteel time. People were nicer."

"Like the English oppression of the Indians and the Africans?"

"Come on, Ben. If you hate Victorians so much, why do *you* come to these meetings?"

Ben looked directly into Mason's eyes. "Because *I'm* trying to repress something, too."

Mason looked back for longer than Ben expected, but he finally looked away and stood up. He started to reach for his watch but stopped himself. "I'm going to get some lemonade."

Ben sat looking at the others milling about, feeling he'd just changed from being Dr. Jekyll to Mr. Hyde. Why *was* he being such a jerk? He decided to behave himself for the remainder of the evening, and he looked on admiringly as other members of the group showed their prized possessions to everyone else.

There was a lovely doily Claire brought, a finely embroidered runner for a dresser that Holly showed off, a porcelain pitcher that Brenna shared. Calder showed everyone a huge photograph of Westminster Palace, pointing out that the gilded wooden frame around the photograph was also Victorian.

"Things were *so* much more beautiful then," Carol murmured.

"And it's here in the Houses of Parliament where same-sex marriage in Britain is going to be determined soon," Calder said.

"Oh, not this again," said Carol. "I propose a new rule. No talking about homosexuality during our meetings. It's too disgusting."

"Do I disgust you, Carol?" Calder asked. Ben looked at Calder sharply.

"You do when you talk of this…this nonsense."

"My brother's gay," Calder stated simply. "And I'll be marching for gay rights this weekend, along with three hundred other active Mormons."

"Three hundred," scoffed Carol. "What's that out of all our millions? You need to repent and get back to living a moral life."

"Next week," Calder went on, ignoring her, "a group of a hundred and fifty Mormons are planning to have a mass resignation from the Church, protesting for gay rights and against polygamy and the Church's treatment of women."

"The Church treats me just fine!" Carol thrust a finger in Calder's direction. Claire and Holly nodded vigorously beside her. "And what's a hundred and fifty, anyway? That's nothing."

Ben was sweating, he was so nervous listening to this exchange. Finally, when there was a brief lull in the conversation, he cleared his throat. "Sometimes, I fear for the future of the Church," he said. "The Church was true at the time of Jesus, and it still failed. If the leaders continue with their out-of-touch policies…" He didn't *want* the Church to fail. Even as a gay Mormon, he liked the Church.

"Don't you worry your pretty little head about it," said Carol. "Now who's next? Calder's done."

The next few Society members spoke in muted tones as they showed their prizes, a finely carved chair, a large photograph of an Indian Head penny, along with an uncirculated specimen in a plastic case, and a piece of china from a Victorian setting. Next came a lachrymatory, a small glass vial containing tears, with a special stopper that allowed the tears to evaporate slowly, so that the person who owned the vial could appropriately end their period of mourning when the tears had dried.

Things livened up a little when a middle-aged couple stood by the window, the husband singing "Oh, My Darling Clementine" and his wife singing "While Strolling through the Park One Day."

But Ben was still upset about all the talk earlier. He knew how most Mormons felt about gays. It was bound to be worse in a group that celebrated an even more repressive culture. Yet Calder had got him thinking. The vows he'd made in the temple only to have sex with his legally and lawfully wedded spouse could still be maintained. Gay marriage was perfectly legal in some states.

That wouldn't keep the Church from excommunicating him, but wouldn't it keep him from Heavenly Father's condemnation?

If only he could know for sure how Mason felt. It was one thing to know Mason was gay, but that certainly didn't mean Mason was in love with him. A gay man didn't love another gay man just because they were both gay any more than any random straight man loved any random straight woman. Even that one erection Ben had stimulated in Mason didn't really prove anything. Sexual excitement and love were two different things.

Someone passed around some Victorian postcards, a woman showed off an authentic Victorian dress, and another woman brought a bustle. A man passed around his twelve-inch replica of the Statue of Liberty, and another man passed around donation envelopes for the Red Cross, which had been established by Clara Barton in Victorian times. This led Calder to quip that eight-hour workdays had also first been proposed during the 1880's.

"And let's not forget the suffragette movement," he added, "which Mormons were behind 100%. In the Victorian era, we were quite progressive. Now, if we could get the Mormon Victorian Society to march in the Gay Pride parade, that would really make news."

Ben noticed Mason fingering his pocket watch through his clothing.

"One more comment like that and we're going to institute a member review policy. No one allowed in the group who isn't living Church standards." Claire and Holly stared icily at Calder. "And that includes fully supporting the Church's proclamations on public morality."

"Now, who's next?" Carol asked, forcing a smile. "I think I saw a pair of beaded shoes around here somewhere."

"It's my turn," Mason said, standing up abruptly. There was something in his tone which made Ben look at him worriedly. Mason handed his copy of Milton to the person at his left, and then he turned to Ben and said sadly, "This will be my last meeting with you guys. I'll really miss you."

"See what you've done!" Holly wagged her finger in Calder's direction.

Mason held up his hand and shook his head. "I'm gay," he said softly, "and I know you guys won't want me around anymore." Ben started trembling, thoroughly scared and yet happy at the same time. For some reason, he thought about Tennyson's comment, "Better to have loved and lost than never to have loved at all," which he remembered the poet had written for another man.

There was silence but only for a few seconds. Then Carol spoke again. "We most certainly do *not* want you here. The whole point of this group is to escape the evils of today's world. I can't believe you're bringing your filth amongst us."

Ben stood next to Mason and put his hand on Mason's arm, his heart beating so hard it hurt. "He's not corrupt," he said, trying to keep his voice from shaking. "He's a virgin, just like I am."

"Bully for you," said Alice, a woman who always wore her hair in a tight bun. A few other members of the group began murmuring as well. Ben realized he had no idea when the bun as a hairstyle had been developed.

"That's right." Ben nodded. "Bully for us. We're going to stay virgins until we get married." He squeezed Mason's hand. "We still believe in the Church, even if the Church doesn't believe in us."

"Oh, my God, are you gay, too?" Carol put her hand to her bosom as if she might swoon. Ben wondered if she were wearing a corset.

"No taking the Lord's name in vain," someone said from across the room.

"See what you're doing?" Carol hissed. "You're bringing us all down!"

Still holding Mason's hand, Ben started to pull him toward the door, directing him to retrieve his book before they left. They drove to Ben's place in silence. After they parked, Ben nodded toward the building, and Mason followed him inside. Ben closed the door behind them and wrapped his arms around Mason.

"I love you," Ben whispered. He felt Mason hug him more tightly.

"What's to become of us?" Mason mumbled into Ben's shoulder.

"We're going to live happily ever after."

Mason pulled away and looked at Ben sadly. "Fairy tales aren't Victorian," he said.

"I never got to finish my Show and Tell." Ben started to unzip his pants.

Mason backed away. "No. You said we were going to be virgins when we married."

"It's just for a second. You're not even going to touch it." Ben finished unzipping and pulled his erect penis out of his garments.

Mason stood staring at it, transfixed. "When—what?"

"Prince Alberts are Victorian," Ben said. "I got this for you. I always hoped…I hoped…"

They stood looking at each other for a long moment, appraising. Then Mason pulled out his pocket watch. "When are we getting married?"

Ben smiled. "Would you rather go to New York or Boston?" He paused. "Iowa?"

"I'd *rather* get married in the Salt Lake temple."

"All in good time." Ben laughed.

"Do you really think we'll ever get to the temple?" Mason looked at Ben worriedly.

"What's the one thing the Victorian era teaches us?" Ben asked.

Mason looked at him blankly.

He pointed to the cover of his book of Victorian tiles, which was still lying on the coffee table. "Beauty endures forever," said Ben softly. "And true love is beautiful in any time." He led Mason over to the sofa. "Now read me some of *Paradise Regained.*"

"It's not Victorian."

"It's timeless." Ben kicked off his shoes and sat at the far end of the sofa, stretching out and putting his feet in Mason's lap. Mason smiled and set the heavy book on top of Ben's feet. He opened it and began reading.

Ben asked himself what Mason would look like with a nipple ring. He smiled and closed his eyes as he listened to Mason's deep, melodic voice. Then he looked at his photo of the Salt Lake temple on the wall and wondered what the Victorian prophet John Taylor would think.

The Contract

"Bishop," I said, trying to keep my voice even, "I need help understanding why Heavenly Father allowed Carter to die." My only son had been murdered a month ago in the basement of our home where we'd set him up in his own apartment. On Mother's Day. Jim, my husband, wouldn't discuss what had taken place. The neighbors looked at us in fear and avoided us. People at church whispered and put on sad faces, but no one would talk to me.

"My Patriarchal Blessing promised me grandchildren," I said, "and that my son would take care of me in my old age. I have a contract with God. I want to know how such a thing could happen."

"Heavenly Father can't stop evil men from being evil," the bishop said in a smooth, comforting voice. It wasn't comforting. "Perhaps you should have had more than one child."

I stared at him.

"What I mean to say," the bishop continued, "is that perhaps you were too close to your son, babied him too much."

"What in the world does that have to do with him being murdered?" I asked in confusion. Priesthood leaders were supposed to be inspired. This man in front of me spent his days as a bank manager. Even the apostles were mostly attorneys and businessmen. Mormon Church leaders could do with a little training. More than just a religion course or two at Brigham Young. "Are you saying if we'd charged him more rent, he'd still be alive?"

Sometimes, I thought my bishop might have Asperger Syndrome, but he seemed to catch my sarcasm. I didn't want to be difficult, but I was under a lot of stress, and he was spewing nonsense.

The bishop closed his eyes and swallowed, looking as if he'd just eaten a raw snake egg. A rotten one at that. "Sister Gibson," he said, "I don't want to make the situation any more difficult for you than it already is, but you must know that your son associated with…unpleasant people."

"My son was a junior at the University of Utah," I replied. "He was an English major."

"So you understand what I'm saying." The bishop looked relieved.

"What in the world are you talking about?" I demanded. I wondered if perhaps I should speak with the stake president instead. Of course, he had no more pastoral training that the bishop, simply the owner of a small chain of restaurants here in Salt Lake.

The bishop sighed, looking as if he now realized he was talking to someone mentally deficient. It was the look he often had when he spoke to me. In the past, I'd just accepted it, but today I wanted to scratch his eyes out. My son had been murdered, and this man was patronizing me.

"Do you know what Carter told me in one of our interviews?" the bishop asked.

"I have no idea," I replied, "since you haven't said *anything* specific yet."

"He told me he learned that Shakespeare wrote love sonnets to another man." He shook his head. "He told me he *liked* those sonnets."

"Everyone likes Shakespeare's sonnets," I replied. "What's your point?"

"Carter told me he read a play by Oscar Wilde. *The Importance of Being Earnest.*"

"I don't understand what you're talking about. Carter read dozens of plays and poems and novels. He was an English major. We already established that."

"Carter told me he liked that play. He told me…he told me it was good and funny. He told me being gay couldn't be a sin because a sinful person couldn't have written something so wonderful." The bishop paused, looking at me as if he'd just added two plus two and was hoping I could make the intellectual leap to come up with the answer all on my own.

"Sister Gibson, your son was becoming corrupt. He started accepting gays. He started thinking like an *intellectual*." He sighed. "He started going down a path that could only lead to destruction."

I smoothed the skirt over my knees. "Bishop," I said carefully, "I came to you for help. My son has been murdered. In his own home. In *my* own home. And you tell me he brought it on himself because he read books?" Now I was beginning to wonder about the bishop's intellect.

"Sister Gibson," the bishop replied, "you're aware, of course, of the covenants we make in the temple?"

"Are you kidding me? I go once a month."

He nodded. "We're making a contract with God. We promise to obey him. We promise…" he said, "we promise to live chaste lives."

My brows furrowed. "Are you telling me my son wasn't chaste?" Now I was confused again. "Carter told me just a week before he died that he was still a virgin." I stopped and took a breath. "He told me he was afraid he'd die a virgin. And he did." The thought made me sad, but I'd promised myself I wouldn't cry in front of the bishop.

"Sister Gibson, you're making this very difficult. I want to honor your son's confidences, but I feel you're pushing me to reveal the true nature of some of our talks."

My son had been a good man. An Eagle scout, a returned missionary who'd been a zone leader in his mission to Maine, Gospel Doctrine teacher in his Singles ward. He went grocery shopping with me every week and helped me understand which products were the best buy, either for price or for quality. He read me poetry during Family Home Evening while Jim was watching Monday Night Football. He still had Family Evening with me, not with the Singles in his ward. He was a good boy.

"Sister Gibson, your son was gay." The bishop breathed a sigh of relief, as if he'd just said something important.

"Well, of course he was," I replied. "I've known that since he was six years old." Was the bishop telling me Heavenly Father had allowed him to be murdered because of *that*? "He was also committed to living the gospel. He was a virgin," I repeated. A mother made the most important contract of all with her children, one literally signed in blood, to watch over them.

I'd made sure Carter was a good man, whatever burdens the Lord had placed on his shoulders. "It's not a sin to *be* gay," I went on. "The Church has said so. It's just a condition, like having epilepsy or being sterile." I bit my lip, remembering how I'd never been able to become pregnant a second time. "A burden the Lord gives to test us."

The bishop shook his head. "Your son came to me many times," he returned, "agonizing over his situation. He said the temptation to sin was too great, that celibacy wasn't an option, that he wasn't strong enough to live an entire life without falling, that he knew he was damned."

I didn't know what to say about this revelation. It seemed unlikely Carter would ever have said such a thing, but surely the bishop wouldn't lie at a time like this. Yet it still didn't explain anything.

"I told him to watch a lot of LDS movies," the bishop said. "I told him to read LDS books." He looked very sad. "And do you know what he told me?" He paused, and I wasn't sure if he was expecting an answer. "He told me they weren't very good. Can you imagine?" He looked as if he were about to try to reach over his huge desk and touch my hand, but then the moment passed. "Your son was corrupt," he repeated.

"Bishop," I said slowly, "I hear words coming out of your mouth, but I don't understand what you're saying. Are you telling me my son was murdered because he didn't like Deseret Book?" I thought back to one of the last activities Carter and I had shared together. We'd watched a DVD of *Sister Act* one evening. I remembered him telling me that since it was about nuns, it couldn't be a sin to watch.

I'd thought it an odd remark at the time, but he must have been feeling guilty for watching any regular movies at all. I wanted to slap the bishop for making him feel that way. The bishop was supposed to be giving him strength, not making him feel like a failure for watching a simple comedy about a church choir. Even if they were Catholics.

"I made your son sign a contract," the bishop continued. "To remain celibate for six months. I was afraid to make the contract any longer than that. I thought we'd take it a day at a time. But Carter came to me not a month after he'd signed it and told me he'd been to a gay bar."

I took in a deep breath.

"He said he didn't go home with anyone," the bishop assured me. "He said he only drank a Coke, but he said he saw a cute guy…" The Bishop swallowed. "And he went home and masturbated." He closed his eyes. "Your son was in serious trouble, Sister Gibson."

I nodded, finally starting to understand the gravity of the situation.

"Your son masturbated all the time. At least twice a week. I hate to have to tell you all this. I don't want to mar the memories you have. But as bishop I have the power of discernment, and I sense you need to know the truth."

I looked down in my lap for a long moment before turning back to the bishop. I picked at a piece of lint on my skirt. "I…I still don't understand," I said. "Are you saying that Heavenly Father let him be struck down because he was evil? You keep telling me he wasn't the good man I thought he was, but I still don't understand how this has anything to do with his being murdered."

The bishop clasped his hands together and blew out a heavy breath. "I don't think you appreciate the severity of your son's depravity. You know he was a stake missionary."

"Yes?"

"He came in to tell me that one night when he was going on splits with one of the elders, the missionary told him he was homesick and cried." The bishop looked very uncomfortable. "The missionary put his head on Carter's shoulder, and Carter hugged him."

I felt uncomfortable, too, but I also felt proud of my son for being decent. It wasn't a sin to be decent.

"Carter came into my office, and *he* cried. He said it was the first time he realized that it was intimacy with another man that he really craved, not just sex. He was heartbroken because the missionary wouldn't talk to him again after that, because he was too embarrassed. Carter was very hurt."

I looked at my lap again. I'd come to the bishop for understanding, and I was finally starting to grasp the bigger picture about my son's life. Maybe the man *was* inspired.

Now I felt sad and hurt and happy and confused. Carter had been a good person. Even all these "revelations" did nothing but prove that.

I was sorry for his pain but grateful he'd remained true to the end. Perhaps Heavenly Father hadn't punished him by allowing him to be murdered but had actually done him a favor, kept him a virgin until the day he died.

"Do you know what your son told me during our last interview?"

It couldn't be bad, I told myself. It couldn't.

"He told me he wanted to kill himself, but he was too chicken. He said he was a failure even at this, and it upset him greatly."

I thanked God that my son had been murdered and hadn't committed suicide, an unpardonable sin. I was glad I'd come to see the bishop. He was making me come to terms with the murder. I saw now it was God's doing. I breathed a sigh of relief. The bishop was a good Latter-day Saint. The Church was a great institution, even with untrained lay leadership. I'd wondered sometimes, but now I knew. The Church was true.

I wished Carter had come to me about all this. I would have read poetry back to him. I could have helped him through it all. That's what mothers were for. I could have been more emotionally intimate with my son, given him what he needed. He would have been okay.

"Carter told me he tried to tell your husband he was afflicted with same-sex feelings," the bishop went on. Now he looked uncomfortable again. "He told me Jim cut him off when he sensed the direction the talk was going, that he said he'd rather hear that his son was dead than that he was gay."

My mouth hung open. The words stung, but that sounded like exactly the kind of thing Jim would say. In fact, now that I thought about it, I remembered Jim had been especially tense and moody that last week before Carter was murdered. He'd slammed doors, broken a plate, been very rough during sex.

Oh, my Lord. "*Jim* didn't kill our son, did he?" I put my hand to my mouth.

"No, no, no, no, no," the bishop said, horrified. He looked up at the photograph of the First Presidency on his wall as if asking for guidance. He seemed to want to crawl underneath his desk rather than go on. But what could there be left to tell? "Carter," he said slowly, as if every syllable pained him, "Carter said that he was a failure even as a gay person because he didn't know any bad people. He told me…he told me…"

"Yes?"

"He told me he was going to go to the sleaziest bar he could find and…"

Oh, my Lord, I prayed, don't let him tell me Carter had sex before he died. Not when he only had a few days left to live. Heavenly Father, please don't let him tell me that.

"Carter said he only had $250 to his name."

"He didn't hire a prostitute, did he?" I asked in horror. Oh, why had I come in to talk to the bishop? Why hadn't I left well enough alone?

"He told me he was going to hire a hit man. Take a contract out on his own life." He shook his head. "Of course, I thought he was joking."

I remembered now what the police had said. Carter had opened his door and been shot immediately in the head. There'd been no robbery, no apparent motive of any kind. They'd asked if Carter had been into drugs but gave up when they found nothing incriminating in his apartment. Nothing except an unsigned love letter. I'd thought it might be from a girl. Finally. But now I suspected the young missionary. Some of the previously vague references now made sense.

"Sister Gibson, your son committed suicide."

I looked the bishop in the face for a long moment, and he looked back. He seemed about to try to reach for my hand again. I looked up at the photo of the First Presidency as he had done. Then I stood up.

"I appreciate you taking the time to talk to me," I said. "I understand everything perfectly now." Carter had given me the best Mother's Day present a child could give his mother. The gift of dying before he was hopelessly lost to the Adversary.

The suicide we could work around, since he hadn't pulled the trigger himself.

It wasn't a sin to make the ultimate sacrifice to protect one's virtue. Girls were told to do so all the time. It had to be true for gay men, too. They were almost like girls, weren't they? "You haven't told the police, have you?"

"I thought it best not to, under the circumstances." He turned his palms upward in supplication. "No sense besmirching your name. Or the Church's."

I nodded. "Thank you, Bishop."

He stood and offered his hand. "Please come talk to me any time you need to," he said.

I shook his hand and started for the door but then turned back. "Well, I've been having some difficulty with one of my teachers in Young Women," I said. "I'd like to talk to you about Sister Bingham sometime."

"Does next Sunday at 1:00 work for you?"

"That'll be fine." I smiled, a weak smile, but my first real one in several weeks. "See you then." I walked out the door, down the hall, and out through the lobby entrance. I climbed into my car and turned on the ignition.

Tonight I wouldn't complain if Jim was rough. I'd made a commitment to him in the temple. I was lucky he was a real man. One always had to defer to the priesthood. I was lucky to have so many good priesthood holders in my life.

Even Carter. Maybe what he did *had* made him a real man in the end.

I thanked Heavenly Father and began humming the melody to "Count Your Many Blessings" as I headed home.

The Three Nephites Get Syphilis

It was 10:00 in the morning on a bright June day when I had my first appointment with Fred, Charles, and Jeff. I was a couples counselor in Salt Lake City, a little disillusioned with the number of Latter-day Saint marriages here in the capital of Mormonism that were in serious trouble. Sometimes, I wondered if there was enough substance in the Church to keep a relationship going.

But I usually did stick to heterosexual couples, since it seemed a foregone conclusion that gay relationships couldn't last. Still, I needed to pay the bills, so when Fred called my receptionist to make the appointment, I had her accept it.

"So Fred," I said as the men sat down. "And Charles. And Jeff. What brings you here today?"

"It's Charles," said Fred. "He cheated on us. Gave us all syphilis. We're very irritated and offended and betrayed."

I nodded. Wasn't that what all gay couples did, I thought. The fact that there were three men in my office rather than two already suggested the degree of their depravity. "Go on," I said.

"We committed to monogamy ages ago," Jeff went on.

"Bigamy," I corrected.

"Whatever," said Fred. "And now we find out Charles isn't satisfied with us. It's humiliating. I don't know if we can go on."

"So why not break up?" I asked. "There's no law saying gays have to make a relationship work when things get bad." Wasn't that the whole problem with gays in the first place? Lack of commitment?

"Who said we're gay?"

I stared at them a moment. "Well, I…uh…are you three in a relationship or not?"

The men looked at each other. Then Fred spoke up. "We talked it over and decided we'd find someone we could trust. We did our research. Even when you were bishop a few years ago, you never revealed any confidences."

"Of course not."

"So we agreed to tell you we're the Three Nephites. We figured you'd understand."

I stared again for a long moment. Then I pretended to write something down in my notebook. The Three Nephites, of course, were three of the twelve Native American disciples of Jesus who followed him when he came to visit the Americas after his resurrection in Israel. Jesus offered the men whatever gift they wanted. Most wanted to live out their lives happily and then ascend to be with him, but three wanted to stay on the Earth and live forever so they could continue to spread the gospel.

People here in Utah sometimes reluctantly gave change to old homeless men, just in case they were Nephites in disguise, testing their moral character.

"And just how did three righteous men end up in a homosexual relationship?" I asked, to keep the conversation going. I didn't know if these guys were delusional or just pulling my leg.

"Oh, it didn't happen for almost three hundred years," Jeff explained.

"I'll tell the story," said Fred.

"Who died and made you boss?"

"No one," grumbled Charles. "No one dies. That's the problem."

"May I *please* continue?" asked Fred. He raised his eyebrows at the others and they quieted down. I nodded at Fred. "So *anyway,* we had wives for a long while. But those were hard times. No medicine. Something goes wrong, and wham, you're gone. So our marriages only lasted twenty, thirty, maybe forty years, sometimes only five." He shrugged. "You lose that many wives over three hundred years, it gets painful."

"Like you ever loved Samoni," muttered Charles.

"She married *me*, didn't she?"

"Go on," I said.

"And it's not just that," Fred continued. "But your kids grow older than you, and they die, too. It's not pleasant. And

I can tell you, they really resented us staying young. Never any inheritance. There was a lot of animosity."

"I can imagine." I thought for a second. "So you guys just live forever, gaining experience and leaving others to die behind you?"

"Haven't you ever seen *Highlander*?" asked Jeff. "Where do you think the writer got the idea?"

"I *told* you not to go blabbing to every guy you have a drink with," said Fred.

"It was a good movie. They didn't have those in the old days."

"What about all the immortals killing each other?"

"That was just wishful thinking," said Charles.

"Well, we do get sick, and we can be injured. We just heal very quickly." Fred gave an annoyed glance at Charles. "But we had syphilis long enough to find out Charles had been unfaithful."

"God, you can be boring."

"Don't take the name of the Lord in vain."

"Guys, guys, we need to focus," I said.

Fred put up both hands as if he were stopping a car. "So finally one day, we were having a picnic, just the three of us, a little ways outside of Zarahemla, and we decided that after our present wives died, we'd just marry each other from then on."

"What a mistake that was." Charles rolled his eyes.

"You'd rather have had forty-five more dead wives?"

"Better dead wives than a live asshole."

"I've willingly given up my asshole thousands, no, *millions* of times for you, when you know I like to be top."

"Let's get back to the topic," I said calmly, pretending to smile, and wondering if I should call 911. "How did you guys get married, or are you disciples of Christ out committing fornication every day?"

"Oh, Alma the Younger came to marry us," Jeff said. "It was a lovely ceremony."

"Alma the Younger?" His account in the Book of Mormon had always been my favorite part.

"Oh, he was resurrected by then. We met him at a brunch shortly after Jesus showed up."

"Nephites had brunches?"

"We were a very advanced people."

"I see."

"Anyway," said Fred, "he gave us a temple wedding. This was not long before the rest of the Nephites apostatized. At least we still had a temple to go to."

"Oh, Fred, he married us outdoors in Bryce Canyon. Don't you remember?"

I held up my hand. "Wait a minute," I said. "You're the Three Nephites, and your names are Fred, Charles, and Jeff?"

"Well, we change them every sixty or seventy years," Fred said defensively. "You get tired of the same name forever and ever."

"That's not all you get tired of," muttered Charles.

"Like your voice," said Fred.

"Like your face," said Charles.

I raised my hand again. "If we're going to solve any issues, we need to be civil in here."

"So as I was saying," Fred began.

"Wait a second," I interrupted. "How did Alma marry you? You're still all men."

"So?"

"So homosexuality is a grave sin."

"Well, as I *said*, we're not gay. This is just situational. But in any event, you people have got it all wrong. There's not a single word in the Book of Mormon against homosexuality. And if you'd read the sealed portion of the book, you'd know that God is irritated when you persecute gays."

"The sealed portion has never been revealed."

"Of course it has. Haven't you heard of Christopher Marc Nemelka? He was finally given permission to translate it. Anyway, the past few decades, we've been trying to minister specifically to gay Mormons, but they've been so hurt they're hard to reach. They could do so much good for the Church if you'd let them. But you guys are so resistant to inspiration. It's going to be a race to see if the Church will fall into apostasy again before the Second Coming."

"Okay, okay. So you're legally married." I sighed. The guys *were* kooks. "I'll just grant it for the sake of argument. But why marry each other if you're not gay? Wouldn't that make sexual relationships…awkward?"

Charles whistled and Jeff groaned.

"I do my best, guys," Fred said petulantly.

"I can only shout 'Teeth!' just so many times."

"I think we need to go back to women," said Charles. "I can't take it any longer. I am *so* sick of dicks."

"I thought you liked mine," said Jeff in a hurt voice.

"Well, considering the alternative." Charles glowered at Fred.

"Maybe they're right," said Fred, looking defeated. "We don't have a specific timeline, but it *can't* be that much longer before Jesus returns. What's that? One or two more wives? We can handle that."

"Now you're talking," said Charles.

"It's just…it's just that…" Fred stumbled.

"What?" I asked.

"If we can't make a relationship work for a mere two thousand years, how are we ever going to live with our wives for a whole eternity?"

I thought of my own dear wife, and how even as Relief Society president, she still had plenty of habits that annoyed me. "Well, if we're *perfect…*" I began.

"Do you know how long it takes to become perfect?" Charles interrupted. "We were starting with good material, and we're nowhere near the goal yet. We'll kill each other long before we become perfect."

I nodded and pretended to write in my notebook again. I was wondering now if instead of being crazy, these guys were simply role-playing, trying to use the Book of Mormon to spice up their sex lives. Mormons might believe in eternal sex, but they were so staid it got old pretty quickly.

I wondered if there were characters my wife and I could play. We'd started bickering more lately, too. "So," I said finally, looking up again. "Do we get Alma to come back and issue you a divorce?" For people like my wife and me, the big D was almost as much of a disgrace as excommunication, but for gay guys like this, it couldn't mean that much.

The men looked at each other. "Well…" said Fred.

"Well…" said Charles.

"I kind of like *your* dick," Jeff said to Charles.

"And I like watching *Glee* with you."

The men looked at each other another few moments. I glanced at my watch.

"I suppose we could try to stay together a *little* longer," said Fred.

"But we'll need to come meet with you at least twice a week," Charles insisted, looking at me intently.

"Can you afford that?" I asked.

"We've got insurance," said Jeff.

"Okay," I agreed, closing my notebook. "I think that's enough for today. Talk to the receptionist on your way out and set up a regular time we can see each other."

We all shook hands, and then Fred and Jeff left the office first. Charles lingered just a moment, and when the others were out of earshot, he whispered, "I've got two thousand years of experience with this baby." He grabbed his crotch. "You don't have any STD's, do you?"

"I'll see you in a couple of days," I said in my most professional tone. Gays, I thought. Charles smiled and joined his friends.

After the three men left, I sat at my desk a long, long while, thinking about what had happened. The guys were beyond role-playing, but I was a counselor, not a psychiatrist, and money was money. Of course, if I was a good Mormon, I had to admit the possibility that their story was true. Wouldn't *not* believing the Three Nephites were real and out there *somewhere* show a lack of faith?

And if their story *was* true, it raised the question of just what kind of arrangements gods made to keep sex interesting after the first three or four million years in the Celestial Kingdom.

I shook my head to clear it, and since I didn't have another appointment for twenty more minutes, I got out my

Book of Mormon and turned to Third Nephi. There weren't many female characters my wife could play, but perhaps she could be the leader of the Gadianton robbers, and I could be Gidgiddoni.

It was the first time I ever got a hard-on from the scriptures.

But that was sure better than falling asleep.

I smiled and kept reading.

A Camouflaged Life

"Mom, why don't you go to church anymore?"

Laverne grimaced as she read the letter from her son in France. She knew the question was bound to come up sometime. Clark had left on his mission well over a year ago, just before Ronald Reagan was elected. Now, a week after a man hiding in the crowd shot the President, Clark was asking personal questions for the first time. Had the assassination attempt made him more philosophical?

Laverne looked at the date on the letter. Air mail from France usually took two weeks to arrive in Georgia, and this letter was no exception. Clark had written this before the shooting. It was completely unrelated.

Was *she* feeling more philosophical?

Laverne continued reading the onion-thin paper. He'd taught one lesson this week in Paris, had an argument with his companion, and been invited in for dinner by a family whose door he knocked on while tracting. The family hadn't been interested, but Clark had tried escargot for the first time. He liked it. He'd come a long way from the timid, picky eater he'd been at home.

Laverne put the letter down. It was Wednesday, and she usually wrote her weekly letter to Clark on Sunday while Murray was reading the Book of Mormon. It made her feel as if she was doing something religious, even though she had gone inactive in the Church five years earlier. Murray never bothered her about why she no longer attended services with him. The bishop hadn't asked her why she quit attending. Her Visiting Teachers never asked.

Maybe nobody cared.

Well, now Clark was asking. She almost welcomed the question.

Though how she was going to answer without revealing the truth to her son, she didn't know.

Laverne got up from the sofa where she'd been sitting. Her Chihuahua, Sandy, jumped out of her lap and looked up at her eagerly, ready to follow. Forty pounds overweight, Laverne sometimes felt her fat was a disguise, heavy gear to wear into battle. She walked slowly up the stairs and down the hallway to her study.

It was tiny, maybe six feet by six. Murray had designed it into the plans when he built the house eighteen years earlier, when the two children were mere toddlers.

Laverne sat at her desk with the letter still in hand. Sandy looked up at her, a little miffed that the comfortable lap was no longer available, and curled up at Laverne's feet. Laverne stared at her typewriter, a manual, the one she'd had for over twenty years now. She'd so wanted to become a writer. Grace Metalious was her hero.

She'd written one short story, a "true confession" about a young woman having an affair with a married man, and submitted it to a magazine, but the editor had sent her a scathing reply, and she'd never had the nerve to submit again.

She wondered if she would be any better at writing now.

"Mom, why don't you go to church anymore?"

Did she dare tell her son the truth? Would he disown her? Would he hate her? He was a good boy as kids went these days, but missions did strange things to people. The Church did strange things to people.

Laverne usually handwrote her letters to Clark. Maybe today she'd type. It would feel as if she were writing a story. Maybe it would be easier to tell that way. She put a sheet of onion paper in the typewriter. She pushed the carriage over and stopped with her fingers poised over the keys.

"Dear Clark, we enjoyed hearing about your week. Things here are about the same. Susan and David are still fighting. We don't expect their marriage to last much longer. But they've made it almost six years now. That's not bad for a marriage that began when your sister was only sixteen."

Susan and David shared Susan's bedroom, and their son, Terrence, slept in the guest room. The couple were trying to save money so they could put a down payment on a home. Laverne kept encouraging them to save just a little more before leaving, thinking a divorce would be easier before a house was involved.

Laverne was sure she'd shocked Clark when she told him why Susan was missing school that day several years ago. She was pregnant and Laverne and Murray had to arrange a wedding quickly. "I think everyone should try out sex before they get married," she'd told Clark. Clark hadn't said anything in return, and Laverne had never directly asked Clark how he really felt about any of it.

Laverne wondered if she would have married Murray at all if they'd had sex first. They'd met in 1956 and dated a year before marrying. They'd kissed and fondled each other, and Murray had dry humped her a couple of times, but they'd never taken their clothes off. Laverne kept thinking, "Maybe this gets better when it's the real thing." Her wedding night proved just as disappointing. "Maybe I'm a slow bloomer," she thought then. "Maybe I'll learn to like it later."

She was certainly a dutiful wife. She never faked headaches or anything like that to get out of sex. She knew her place. She cooked and cleaned and lay back in silence for Murray. The oral sex was a little harder to fake. In the last few years, she'd bought books about sex, including one called *The Happy Hooker*, hoping to learn some tips. Surely, hookers didn't really enjoy everything they were doing, but they learned to be convincing. That was what she still hoped to do.

"Terrence is enjoying kindergarten and really looking forward to first grade in the fall," Laverne typed. "Your dad is busy building houses, so there's plenty of money. You won't have to come home early. Everything here is fine."

Laverne looked at the letter jutting out of the typewriter. No wonder the editor had blasted her writing. It was utterly boring. She had to *say* something.

"You asked why I don't go to church any longer," she continued typing, her fingers tingling with anticipation. "I don't really know what to tell you." She thought about offering a white lie, or saying she'd tell him when he returned home, or just making up something completely out of the blue. "I used to have a testimony," she kept typing. "I used to believe the Church was true. I don't want to discourage you from enjoying your missionary work, but I simply don't believe anymore. I just don't feel anything anymore when I pray."

Laverne stopped again and reread the last few lines. Would Clark bear his testimony to her in return? Would he berate her? Would he feel disappointed she'd lost her way? She couldn't bear to have Clark be disappointed in her. And this mission really was helping him come out of his shell. She didn't want to do anything that might jeopardize his time in France. She wanted him to experience life.

Laverne shifted her feet and accidentally kicked the Chihuahua. Sandy yelped and jumped up, and then curled up again with a stern look and a heavy sigh. Laverne reached down to give the dog a quick pat of apology.

"To tell you the truth, Clark, the fact is that I can't see myself spending an eternity with your father. I don't want to, and I don't expect he does, either. But don't worry. It's not that we want to divorce or anything. It's just that—"

Laverne reached down and picked up Sandy, setting her gently on her lap. It was a little awkward reaching the typewriter without crushing the dog, but sometimes, she felt that this little creature was the only one who really understood her. She always barked at Murray, always barked at David, and merely tolerated Susan and Terrence. Sandy did appear to like Clark a little bit.

But she had always liked Laverne best.

She rubbed the dog behind the ears. Sandy closed her eyes in pleasure. Why couldn't people have the pure souls that dogs did? No pretense. What you see is what you got.

"Well, perhaps you *should* worry," Laverne typed. "I don't suppose this is the best way to tell you, but I'm not attracted to your father." She hesitated. "I'm not attracted to any man. What I want is to be with another woman. But I won't leave your father until after you come home from your mission. Probably not until you finish college. And maybe not even after that. I've never been with another woman, but I find it difficult to make friends with other women. I enjoy their company too much.

"I haven't told your father or your sister or anyone else. Not even the bishop. If you feel you have to tell them, I'll understand. But I think life is hard enough without everyone else knowing.

"Still, you asked, so I'm answering. If the Church were true, God could make me love your father. If the Church were true, God would allow me to love a woman. If the Church were true, the last twenty-two years of my life wouldn't have been pure hell."

Did she sound too melodramatic? That boor of an editor so many years ago had used the term.

"I tried very hard for several years after the missionaries converted us back when you were twelve. I thought I just had to give it time. But I can't give it my whole life. So when your father goes to church on Sunday, I go next door and spend time with Agatha. I love Agatha. She's married, too, with three kids, and we haven't done anything more than talk.

But even just talking to her is more rewarding than anything I've ever done with your father. And more rewarding than anything I've ever felt at church."

She took a deep breath.

"I feel terrible telling you these things, and yet I feel strangely happy, too. Perhaps I'm cheating by saying this in a letter rather than waiting to face you in person when you get home.

"Clark, don't argue with your companion. Accept him as he is, faults and all, even if he doesn't accept you. Be the bigger man and enjoy your time in France as much as you can. Too soon, you'll have to come back and face the tedium of life in Atlanta. Have an adventure while you have the chance."

Laverne pulled the sheet of typing paper out of the typewriter. She had single-spaced it, but she was still near the bottom of the page, much longer than her usual empty letters. She picked up a pen and signed, "Love, Mom" and then folded it up and addressed an overseas envelope.

She couldn't mail it till morning, and she was already anxious to hear Clark's reply, though he wouldn't even receive the letter for two more weeks, and then would have to wait till Preparation Day before he could reply, and she'd have to have still two weeks after that before his letter arrived in America.

But maybe she would have talked to Murray by then. That might be for the best anyway. There was no point talking to the bishop or anyone else. Murray deserved to know, and yet, knowing would hurt his feelings. He always thought he had such sexual prowess. Was it a sin to let him go on believing that?

Laverne reached in her drawer and tore off an air mail stamp. She licked it and placed it on the envelope. She took another deep breath and then sealed the envelope. She was going to mail that letter first thing tomorrow morning.

She picked up Sandy and carried her to the bedroom. It would still be another few hours before Murray came home at 5:15. He left the worksite at 5:00 on the dot every day, and dinner was always waiting for him when he opened the door.

Laverne liked to experiment with Chinese dishes and French dishes and Greek dishes, but Murray was a meat and potatoes man. He'd allow stuffed artichokes sometimes, and maybe Brussels sprouts on occasion, but Laverne had to cook standard fare most of the time. She had two hours before she needed to worry about that today.

Her copy of *Death Has a Small Voice* by Frances and Richard Lockridge lay on her bedside table. It was a husband-and-wife detective series written by a husband and wife writing team.

What might life have been like if she could have ever had a real partner?

Laverne made herself comfortable on the bed with two pillows behind her back. She let Sandy settle in her lap, petted her gently another time, and opened her book. Mr. and Mrs. North found another clue and moved closer to solving the murder. The most exciting thing Laverne ever did was mash some potatoes. Clark got to see the Louvre and the Eiffel Tower. Laverne only got to skip out of church.

There *had* to be something more to life.

What if…what if she *proposed* to Agatha? They were both housewives with no skills. How could they ever make a life together, even if Agatha wanted it as much as she did? Laverne was fully prepared to be a waitress or secretary or whatever else she could do, if she could just be happy, even simply have a *chance* at happiness.

Maybe she could get a job as a prep cook at a Chinese restaurant and learn how to cook authentic Chinese meals. Even working in a Mexican restaurant, where the language barrier might not be as great, could be interesting.

Why, that wasn't a bad idea at all.

Unless Agatha only thought of her as the next-door neighbor and nothing more. But even if that were the case, finally getting it all out in the open would be liberating. Even with a broken heart, she'd feel happier than she did now. Her heart wasn't broken at the moment, but it wasn't whole, either. It was simply a cold, unbeating lump in her chest.

Laverne looked down at her bosom and saw flowers on her dress. But they weren't real flowers, only colored threads in a pattern.

If she stayed with Murray, perhaps when Clark finished his mission in another seven months, they could go to France to pick him up. She could see some of the world herself. And yet, it would feel like looking at a counterfeit Mona Lisa.

She could never experience "the world" until she was honest about who she was and who she loved. Life without authenticity felt like walking about in a thick fog all the time. She simply couldn't detect any firm outlines.

Maybe the Church *was* true and she just couldn't feel it, the way she couldn't feel anything at all while living a camouflaged life.

That thought excited her so much Laverne jerked in the bed, startling Sandy and making her get up and move over to Murray's pillow. Since she hadn't mailed the letter yet, perhaps if she talked to Agatha today, she could write an entirely different letter to Clark in the morning.

Laverne put her book aside and stood up. She was wearing a housedress, plain, little more than a sack. It was comfortable, but you could hardly even tell she was a woman underneath it. She felt as if she were hiding behind frumpiness. Whenever she went next door to Agatha's, though, she put on something with a waistline.

Laverne's waist was nothing she cared to accentuate, but she threw on her most stylish blouse and skirt, briefly fixed her hair, and walked down the stairs. She filled a measuring cup with sugar and headed out the door.

No one answered her knock for the longest time, and Laverne began to have second thoughts. She was just about to turn away when the door finally opened. "Laverne!" Agatha said, her eyes twinkling. "How are you?" Agatha was six years younger than Laverne and thirty pounds lighter.

"I'm fine."

"What's that?"

"A cup of sugar."

"You're supposed to *ask* for a cup, not bring a cup over unasked for." She laughed.

"I like to do things differently."

"Well, come in. Come in." Agatha opened the door more widely and motioned for Laverne to enter.

Laverne looked at her watch. It was 3:30. Agatha's kids would be home from school any minute. Terrence would be home soon, too. She felt her heart pounding in her chest. What was she thinking, coming over here like this?

"I want to go to France," she said finally, feeling she was going to choke on the words.

"How wonderful." Agatha started to pour some lemonade into a glass.

"With you."

Agatha almost spilled the lemonade but put the pitcher down carefully. The glass was barely a third full. "With—without our husbands?" she asked faintly.

"I want to live with you," Laverne blurted out breathlessly, "without our husbands."

Agatha sat down at the kitchen table and stared at Laverne. Laverne thought she was going to die. But at the same time, she'd never felt more alive. It almost didn't matter what Agatha said.

Almost.

"Do you realize what you're saying?" Agatha finally managed to whisper.

Laverne nodded.

Agatha grabbed the glass of lemonade and drank it in one gulp, as if it were a shot. She looked at Laverne, her brows furrowed. "What—? How—?"

"Murray will give me the house. It's almost paid for. Your husband will pay you child support. I'll go out tomorrow morning and get a job in a restaurant."

Agatha poured herself another glass of lemonade. She didn't offer any to Laverne. She drank this one slowly. Laverne was dying. The kids would be home any minute.

"Laverne, I'm going to have to think about this." Agatha stood up.

Laverne stood up, too, smiling. Agatha hadn't said no! She hadn't been repulsed!

Life was *wonderful*!

She went to the door with Agatha, and just as she was about to leave, Agatha leaned forward and gave her a quick kiss on the lips.

Was *this* what everyone else was experiencing all the time? Laverne would have been mad if she wasn't so happy. All this time, she could have been living a real life. But it wasn't too late.

This must be what Joseph Smith felt, she suddenly realized, when he was told all the churches of his time weren't true, but that Heavenly Father would reestablish the true church through him. The whole world living through fake religion, and then suddenly there was the real thing. The story of the restoration made sense again, the way it had eight years ago. Laverne felt as if she were having a revelation herself.

She hurried back to the house, opening the door just moments before the school van carrying Terrence dropped him off. Laverne fixed him a small snack and then let him watch his afternoon cartoons.

She went back upstairs to her study and tore up the letter she'd written to Clark. A wasted stamp. Oh, well. What was that compared to a wasted life? She put another sheet of onion paper into the typewriter so she could begin another letter.

Laverne looked at the blank piece of paper for a long time. Suddenly, she didn't feel like writing to her son anymore. Not yet. There were too many thoughts, too many ideas flying around her head. She'd never felt such energy before. Was this what the second birth, the gift of the Holy Ghost, was like? She felt as if she could stand up and prophesy.

If she couldn't do that, maybe she'd write something, perhaps a mystery, just a short story to get started, not a novel yet. She could never think of any ideas before, but now they were flowing everywhere all around her.

Laverne took out the onion paper and put in a regular sheet, adjusting the top edge. She looked at the blank page a long moment and then started typing. "A shot rang out." She paused to look at the first line. A nice beginning. There was nothing wrong with melodrama. She smiled and started typing some more.

The Land of Desolation

I wanted to go to the Arctic Circle, but I didn't have the money. An organization gathered teachers, scientists, architects, and artists twice a year to embark on a sailing vessel in the Arctic for three weeks. I so wanted to apply for the program, only it cost a staggering $5800, far more than I could afford on my teaching salary. Rob offered to help pay, but even together, we couldn't manage it.

Rob bit into another slice of yellow squash. "Well, Press, couldn't we just go to northern Alaska on our own for a couple of weeks?" he asked. Though my name was Prescott, he never called me that.

"It wouldn't be the same." I scooped up a mouthful of a quinoa and rice, covered with cream of celery gravy. "On the ship, there will be all that talk about climate change, all that interaction with the scientists. What are *we* going to do by ourselves? Sit outside in our shorts and read a book about global warming, fighting off mosquitoes and bemoaning the state of politics in the world?"

"How would physically being on the ship make any difference? Would you suddenly be able to change anything that you can't change now?"

I put down my fork. "I don't want logic," I said. "I want to know how I can solve the world's problems."

"We already don't eat meat because it uses more resources than raising crops. We already keep our thermostat at 55 in the winter."

"But how can I convince *others* that the problem is serious?" I insisted.

Rob chewed another slice of squash. "You can't," he said simply. "But you can give money to organizations that do. You can write to your senators and your representatives and your mayor. You can volunteer with a conservation group or something."

My jaw tightened. "We live in Seattle. Our mayor used to work for the Sierra Club. Our senators and representatives are among the most liberal in the country. I need to reach *other* people." I looked at the rice and quinoa on my plate, and my appetite faded away. Unusual for me.

"Press, you're going to make yourself sick again. Just do your part and don't worry about the rest."

"My part's not enough!" I got up from the table and walked to the sink, though I already had a full glass of water at my seat. "How can the President act like it *doesn't matter*?"

"Just be glad Romney didn't win."

His mention of Romney succeeded in distracting me, and we talked about Romney's pathetic positions and his continual lying, even though lying was considered a serious sin by the LDS Church. Rob and I had both grown up Mormon, Rob in Utah and me in Colorado, and while most of the time we felt we'd moved beyond our residual ties to the Church, things like Romney's candidacy had brought back the full weight of that baggage.

We finished our meal, and I served us each one doughnut I'd bought on the way home from teaching at the high school. Rob liked maple bars, and my favorite was the old-fashioned glazed. I only brought doughnuts home on Friday, though sometimes I cheated earlier in the week and bought one just for myself. I'd let my weight get out of control, up to 210 pounds.

A year and a half ago, I'd gotten in an argument with two elders who'd come to our door and suffered a mild heart attack. My doctor told me I simply had to lose weight, and though the task seemed insurmountable, I started serving smaller portions, making myself walk more, and cutting out most desserts.

Somehow, I managed to lose thirty-five pounds since then, though I still had at least fifteen more to go if I expected to return to my weight of two decades ago when Rob and I first met. If it weren't for Top Pot doughnuts, I probably would already have reached my goal weight by now.

Sometimes, when walking down the street or buying groceries or standing at the bus stop, I'd see some terribly obese man weighing maybe three or four hundred pounds, and I'd think, "At what point did his 'having a problem' with his weight become something that was hopelessly out of control?"

Even if the man were to adopt a strict routine and somehow succeed at losing a pound every single week without fail, it would still take him *years* at that steady pace to make a difference. Did he give up because the job seemed too daunting? Or did he just not care about the consequences?

Most likely, he was simply too weak to do what he knew he needed to do. What he even truly *wanted* to do. I'd see those guys and pray to Heavenly Father not to let the same thing happen to me.

Yet I knew it wasn't up to Heavenly Father to answer that prayer. It was up to me. Still, I knew that Satan could come up with some devilish temptations. A chocolate and peanut butter Easter egg could destroy anybody's will.

To be perfectly honest, part of the reason I wanted to go on this three-week trip to the Arctic Circle was to force myself to give up Top Pot for at least a month. I figured I could add three days before and maybe three days after to the length of the trip itself. No, I couldn't count on being strong enough to keep it up for three days after returning. It would have to be a whole week before leaving. Yes, that would do it.

Of course, it was a moot point now.

The next day, Saturday, I spent the morning grading papers while Rob vacuumed the house. Then we went grocery shopping and bought a couple more yellow crooked neck squash. Nothing tasted better than fried squash. We'd spray the pan with Pam and not use any other oil to fry with. I felt healthy every time I ate the delicious things.

If only we didn't buy the ice cream, too. Just for Saturday night, but still.

"Rob, let's try the frozen Greek yogurt instead."

"It won't taste like ice cream, you know."

"That's okay. It's low fat. And high in protein. With no added sugar. We're always looking for ways to increase our protein intake."

"All right." Rob put the Cookies N Cream back and picked up some frozen vanilla yogurt. "Brrrr. It's cold in here."

"I like it," I said.

"We're not setting the thermostat any lower." Rob grinned, but we'd already discussed the ethics of our thermostat setting. If I didn't *mind* living in a 55-degree house, did my sacrifice really count toward my spiritual welfare? "Is it a sacrifice if you like it?" Rob had asked.

"I still give $75 to American Forests every paycheck, don't I? And another $50 to Save the Redwoods. That's still a sacrifice."

We'd fought over that, too. Due to years of carefree living, we'd both racked up high credit card debt. Rob had been the first to recognize the seriousness of the situation and demand we pay down the cards. It had seemed overwhelming at first.

Rob had over $11,000 on his Mastercard, and I had two Visas, one with an $8000 balance and another with $5500. After almost five years with no vacations and no new electronics and no new much of anything, we'd finally gotten our balances back to zero.

Five years was a long time to go without having fun and eating only cheap food. I suppose we were lucky we stopped ourselves before we owed even more. I'd read articles about people who owed $25,000 or $30,000 on their cards. It must have been hard to start behaving responsibly when one's finances seemed so hopeless to begin with.

Once I no longer needed to make such huge payments every month, I started donating to my favorite charities again. Rob felt we should be building our savings instead. "The environment can't wait," I'd replied. "What good does it do to have $50,000 in savings if the world is coming to an end?"

"We can't save the whole world," he replied. "We have to save ourselves first."

So I didn't tell him I donated to the Sierra Club and the American Chestnut Society and a couple of other conservation groups as well.

Rob put the frozen yogurt into our shopping cart. "Sacrifice is giving up something good for something that's better," he said. "I suppose giving to worthy causes does count."

We made our way to the checkout, and I pretended I didn't see the Reese's peanut butter cups on sale, Buy One Get One Free. I used to do most of the grocery shopping by myself, but I'd learned I needed a chaperone to protect me from the damned checkout aisle.

A drunk with strong breath stopped us at the door, asking for money. "Sorry," I said as we kept moving toward the car.

Back home, after we put away the food, I grabbed another handful of papers and went to the front porch to grade. "It's cold out there," Rob said.

I wanted to enjoy it while I could. "I have my coat on."

Cold was a relative term, of course. It was only about 42 degrees. Seattle never got extremely cold, and last year the winter had been quite mild. I hoped we weren't in for a repeat. Most people liked warm weather, but not only did I prefer the cold, I also felt an indescribable sense of worry and despair every time we experienced another record high temperature. My Mormonism kept haunting me, predicting the end of the world by complete global annihilation.

Mormons didn't particularly believe in climate change as doctrine, just in wide scale disaster, storing up at least a year's supply of food and other necessities to prepare. What if there really were something to prophecy? Rob had been traveling on business many years ago when he woke up one night in his hotel room from a horrifying nightmare that his partner was burning to death.

He thought the dream was sparked by his lingering internalized homophobia, but he learned in the morning that his house had caught fire the night before, and his partner had indeed died. There *was* something to the psychic, the supernatural. If we could see what was happening hundreds of miles away when it happened, could there not be someone, a "real" prophet, who could somehow see into the future as well, at least on occasion? Such a phenomenon, after all, didn't mean there was a god.

But if it were already predicted that the world would "end by fire," did that mean there was nothing which could be done about it? The prediction also included that there would be untold amounts of wickedness in the Last Days. Did that mean we shouldn't still try to be righteous ourselves, or try to convince others to be righteous, too? Surely, we had to fight evil and fight disaster in any way we could, even if it was a losing battle.

I wished I could go to the Arctic Circle.

I remembered Helaman from the Book of Mormon. One of my favorite scriptures while I was still active in the Church was from chapter three: "Yea, and even they did spread forth into all parts of the land, into whatever parts it had not been rendered desolate and without timber, because of the many inhabitants who had before inherited the land….And the people who were in the land northward did dwell in tents, and in houses of cement, and they did suffer whatsoever tree should spring up upon the face of the land that it should grow up, that in time they might have timber to build their houses, yea, their cities, and their temples, and their synagogues, and all manner of their buildings."

It wasn't *exactly* the voice of conservation. The Nephites only wanted to reforest the land so they could use up all the resources again. But it was something *close* to an ecological consciousness. And Joseph Smith had written that in his early twenties, around 1829, when almost no one, not even learned scientists, were much worried about irreversible damage to the environment.

Had Joseph Smith really been inspired?

Maybe I could sell my Vespa, I thought, to raise money for the trip.

Only I liked my Vespa. And Rob didn't want to give up the car just yet, even though we both rode public transportation a great deal.

I still had grading left, but I needed a break and went inside to watch some MSNBC. The reports were still trickling in about Hurricane Sandy's terrific blow to the northeast, weeks after the storm had passed. "This is the wave of the future," a woman told a journalist. "We have to face facts." They'd said the same thing after Katrina seven years earlier, and no one had done anything then, either. What would it take to wake people up?

"I'm going for a walk," I said.

"Okay, hon."

I took my usual route, down half a block, right for three blocks, left for four more, and so on. I picked the route that made me climb the fewest hills. At one corner, I had a view over Lake Washington. The sight never grew old, tree-covered hills rising up across the water, with snow-capped mountains in the background.

Yes, there were a lot of houses on those hills, but there were a lot of trees, too. On some of the hills, I could see the effects of clear cutting, but most still had vegetation.

I always had two simultaneous reactions when I saw the vista. I was of course awed by the incredible beauty before me, right there where I lived. I didn't even need to go on vacation to see it. But at the same time, those one or two clear-cut fields both scared and saddened me. How much longer did we have left? I felt as if I were tied down, watching a murderer creep slowly toward me, step by step.

I wished I could buy some of that clear-cut land and reforest it myself, but that would cost far, far more than a trip to the Arctic.

Whatever the country had spent on the wars in Iraq and Afghanistan, it had to be substantially more than the amount put into green energy and conservation. We *could* do the right thing if we wanted. We could develop more public transportation. We could encourage bicycle riding. We could put higher taxes on vehicles. We could plant more trees. We could invest more in solar energy, in wind, in waves. We could do all this and so much more. We had the ability. It was merely a matter of will.

I changed direction now and went down the hill. I usually tried to stay on level ground during my walks. Every hill I went down meant a hill I had to climb again on my way back. Sometimes, I brought my bus pass so I could ride back uphill. Today, I stopped at the convenience store at the bottom of the hill and bought a Twinkie. Rob didn't have to know.

I stood outside, feeling like a criminal, as I tore open the plastic and took my first bite. Twinkies were going out of production soon. They'd be extinct before long. A man walked by, looking at me. I kept eating.

The blasted thing didn't even taste very good.

I ate the last bite.

Just as I did, I saw the bus go by. Good. I'd have to walk back. Served me right. I walked slowly, telling myself I wasn't in a race, but long before I reached the top, my chest was hurting. I took a couple of breaks and made it without further difficulty.

"Ready for Scrabble?" Rob asked when I walked in the door. Every Saturday afternoon, we took time to play a game.

"Let me grade just one more paper first."

Rob nodded, and I hurried through the grading, a never-ending battle. Sometimes, doing a good job involved an awful lot of tedium. I set up the Scrabble board and called Rob. He walked back into the living room with a smile. "Here's where my advanced degree comes in handy."

"Here's where my work in the halls of education comes in handy."

We played for an hour. Rob usually won, not so much because of his vocabulary but because he made clever use of the double word score and triple word score. I'd leave the triple word score open if it meant I could get a great word somewhere else. I was after the words; he was after the score. He'd put down "nut" and I'd add "pea" to the front of it. His "read" became my "bread." He'd set down "lose" and I'd change it first to "close" and then a turn later to "closer."

Rob won by 47 points.

We listened to a CD of Adele while Rob dusted and I graded the last of my papers.

After dinner, it was time for "date night." We usually watched something on Turner Classic Movies or checked out a DVD from the library. We'd given up Netflix a few years ago and put the extra cash toward our credit cards, and we found that the library was almost, though not quite, as good. We'd tried to give up cable but simply couldn't bear it. The cable bill, even the most basic we could live with, still cost a whopping $78 a month.

It was an outrageous waste of money. I could've planted seventy-eight trees a month with American Forests for that. But we were still selfish and, to be perfectly honest, spoiled.

"I'm a little hesitant to suggest our show for tonight." Rob sat beside me but kept the remote away.

"What is it?" I tried reaching for the remote.

"PBS has a documentary about the Dust Bowl by Ken Burns."

"Sounds perfectly dreary." I smiled.

"You up to it?"

"If we can talk about the Arctic Circle again afterward."

"Do you want to ask your father for the money?"

"Heavens, no." I shook my head. Every time I talked to Dad, he'd ask if I had AIDS yet. "It's only a matter of time," he'd say. "Actions have consequences." I didn't talk to him often.

Rob and I cuddled on the sofa and watched the two-hour first part of the documentary. I'd obviously heard about it growing up, but I had no idea of the degree of man-made damage we'd caused. Destroying the natural vegetation of the area and plowing up millions of acres, combined with a naturally occurring drought, had devastated the region, blowing away nearly five billion tons of topsoil that would never return, even after the rains did.

Not five billion pounds—five billion *tons*. Two dust storms alone one year were estimated to have carried away

650 million tons, and there were dozens and dozens of dust storms each year for several years.

It was unfathomable. Even more surprising was that we as a nation had somehow dealt with it, even during a major economic depression.

And yet what we were facing now was essentially the same kind of devastation, only on a global rather than a local scale. Because our carbon dioxide emissions were raising the Earth's temperature, pine beetles were moving further north and decimating forests, leading to even faster rises in carbon dioxide.

The resulting higher temperatures were leading to droughts covering tens of thousands of square miles of farmland. Lakes and rivers and aquifers were drying up. We were on the brink of a global Dust Bowl.

And politicians were fighting over whether to raise taxes on people earning more than a million dollars. They were arguing over whether to raise the minimum wage. They were attacking each other over whether the government should pay for birth control.

It sounded like two distinguished gentleman aboard the Titanic arguing over a game of cards thirty minutes before their encounter with an iceberg.

I wanted to go to the Arctic Circle. I wanted to be like Christa McAuliffe and make a difference. Only she hadn't really had a chance to make a difference. NASA had been perfectly aware of the problem with their O rings and had sent her into space regardless, as if ignoring a problem could make it go away, that denying responsibility—and reality—wouldn't catch up with them.

We had so much information and were still doing practically nothing. The media even reported on climate change denial as if it were a legitimate scientific position and not a financially motivated one.

As if a worldwide environmental collapse wouldn't cost more than averting one.

I wondered if I could get a video camera like Ken Burns and make a documentary of my own. But what could I say that gifted people like Burns or Al Gore hadn't already said? The problem wasn't a lack of knowledge. Something had to happen that would deny people the option of refusing to face the truth. I was afraid, though, that this "something" would be a disaster too crippling for humans to recover from.

"Are you okay?" Rob asked when the show was over.

I took a deep breath. My chest hurt. "I feel like one single tiny grain of sand in just one of those massive dust storms. What difference can *I* make?"

"Maybe," Rob said softly, "maybe we have to face the fact that we *can't* make a difference. Humans may simply not be smart enough to survive. We'll bring a lot of other species down with us, but the Earth itself will go on, just like it has after other huge extinction events."

I stood up to get a cup of tea. My chest hurt. I rubbed it, and my left arm started tingling painfully. I wanted to deny what Rob had said. I wanted to discover some truth that I'd been missing. I wanted *the answer*.

My arm was now hurting outright, and my chest tightened. An oppressive weight suddenly slammed into my rib cage. I turned to my husband, falling to my knees. "Call—call—"

Rob jumped up and ran for the phone.

It was several days, of course, before I could leave the hospital. They'd put a stent in last time, but this time, the doctor had to do a bypass. It was nasty and ugly and painful. I confessed my cheating, which of course the doctor had been perfectly aware of, just from the lab results.

"You have to stop pretending that eating one extra doughnut won't add to your cholesterol." She shook her head. "In fact, you have to stop pretending that allowing even the one doughnut a week is still okay. You can't have *any* anymore."

I sighed. "But what kind of life will I have without doughnuts?" I looked at the balloons some of my students had brought to the room. Their cheery presence seemed incidental.

"Life," she said.

I nodded.

"You're lucky your Day of Reckoning wasn't final."

Rob picked me up when I was finally released. I wondered if *he'd* still sneak doughnuts now that they were illegal inside the house. "Please don't leave me," he said, helping me into the Prius in the parking garage. "I need you in my life."

He didn't, of course. He could find another, better man easily. I was no grand prize.

"Maybe this year we should try going on vacation again," I said. "Go someplace nice. Relax and enjoy the world." I almost added, "while it's still here," but now was the time to be positive, I decided. I smiled and held Rob's hand after he got behind the wheel.

Rob fingered the red ignition button but didn't press it. His expression became serious as he turned to me. "I sold my stamp collection," he said. "I haven't been able to keep up with the new stamps the past few years anyway."

"But why? You love your stamps."

"I only got $500 for it." He shook his head. "All those stamps. For all those years. A lifetime of effort."

"Rob…"

"We'll need it for our deductible," he went on. "But I've made a decision, an irreversible one."

"What?" I asked warily. An elderly couple toddled past on the way to their car.

"I took out a cash advance on my credit card. $6000."

"What!"

"You're going to the Arctic Circle, Press."

My chest started hurting again. I wanted to rub it but was afraid to.

"It'll even help my credit score." He laughed, shaking his head. "There's always an incentive to live recklessly."

"But it *is* reckless, Rob. Why?"

He shrugged. "Who knows how much longer we have on the planet? We've got to make the most of our lives while we can, whatever the cost." A young couple walked by our row of cars, their little girl running on ahead.

"Wouldn't it be more effective to put all that money toward planting six thousand more trees?"

Rob shook his head. "It's more important for you to feel you matter. We can't succeed at all if we don't manage to feel relevant."

I kept my grasp on Rob's hand. "But it's so—so foolhardy—we'll have to pay it back someday, and—" A horn honked distantly somewhere in the garage.

"Is it any more foolhardy than drilling for oil day after day?" He paused. "There's always a way to turn the tide if we put our hearts into it."

"My heart isn't so great." I shook my head wistfully, forcing a smile.

"With no more doughnuts, and a solid exercise routine, you'll be back to your old self in no time."

"My 'old' self is right." I managed a laugh.

"We can't turn back the clock. But we can make what time we have left worth living." He leaned over and kissed me. "The money is in the savings account. As soon as you get accepted into the program, you can pay the sponsors." He pushed the button to start the car.

Was this our gift of the Magi? Throwing away money to accomplish nothing of value?

"I love you, Rob." I leaned back in my seat and watched a young woman in scrubs heading for the hospital. "I just hope they accept someone with HIV."

"Your T-cells have been fine for fifteen years. Don't worry about it."

We pulled out of the garage and onto the street, and as we drove slowly along, other cars whizzed by us, a Hispanic woman waited for a bus, and a yardful of kids played beside an elementary school. We passed a bakery and my heart skipped a beat.

Overhead, a long stream of crows headed to a destination only they knew. My eyes were drawn to a large billboard showing a pair of outstretched hands and the message, "Are you ready for Judgment Day?"

Not yet, I thought, as I watched Rob concentrate on the road. He turned to me for a moment and smiled. Not yet.

We passed a gas station with a sign advertising gasoline for $3.69. Three cars were at the pumps.

"Wow," said Rob. "$3.69. That's a good deal."

My chest began to hurt again. I sighed and closed my eyes.

The Eyes of March

There was a sudden lurch, and suddenly, the car was in the water. "Oh my god!" Betty screamed. She'd been driving. "We're in the lake!"

Water was already coming up over our feet, quickly. It was ice cold. Water this far north didn't heat up by late March.

"Roll down your window!" I shouted. I rolled mine down and undid my seat belt. By now, the water was up to my waist.

"Oh my god!" Betty yelled. "Oh my god! Dennis, help!"

I pulled myself out the window and looked back inside. Betty still had her seat belt on. Her window was still rolled up. "Betty! Undo your seat belt and get out my window! Hurry!"

"Oh my god! Oh my god! Help me, Dennis! Help!"

The water was up to Betty's neck. The car was almost completely underwater. Betty's eyes were terrified, wild and searching. She was still gripping the steering wheel. I took a deep breath and stuck my head under the water to see if I could reach in and unbuckle her. But the freezing water made it impossible to hold my breath. I pulled back out and took a deep gulp of air. The car was now beneath the surface of the lake.

I took one more breath and ducked under the water again, trying to find the car. It was dusk up above, foggy and misty. I couldn't see anything at all below the surface. And my lungs were screaming for air again. I swam up and breathed in deeply. "Betty! Betty!" I yelled.

I could see a ramp leading down to the water about ten feet away and swam for it. It was difficult climbing up, my hands and legs already going numb. "Help!" I shouted.

A man in a park ranger uniform came running. "Mr. Bantam! You all right?"

"My wife's still in the car!"

The ranger reached down and helped me up the last few feet. Then he called for help on his walkie talkie. What was wrong with him? Why didn't he go in after Betty? Just how long did he think she'd be able to hold her breath?

I lay on the ground, panting, knowing in my heart God was up above, looking down on us. He was a god of love, tender and merciful. I struggled to my feet and looked out onto the black water. Things happened for a reason.

"Betty!" I called again, but the look the park ranger gave me made me feel foolish.

Fifteen minutes later, another Park Service car pulled up, and some men shone a flashlight into the lake. No one went into the water. I stood there shivering, watching them.

"It's too dark to dive," one of the men said calmly. "We'll have to wait till morning."

Even I knew at this point there was no hurry.

"Come on, Mr. Bantam," said the first ranger. "We'll take you to town and find you a hotel."

Betty and I had come to the park for a hike on our thirty-second anniversary. We'd met at BYU years ago and married four months later. Betty was from Salt Lake and I was from New Orleans. That's why I knew how to get out of a sinking car and she didn't. We had the Destrehan-Luling ferry disaster, where seventy-eight people drowned in their cars when a ship hit a ferry crossing the Mississippi River.

We had bridges over lakes and canals that were hit by boats and barges, plunging drivers into the water. The news always carried segments on how to get out of a sinking car. Even after Betty was submerged, she still could have gotten out if she'd known how.

Why hadn't I ever gone over this in Family Home Evening? We lived in Bangor. There was water all over the place here, like this lake. Why hadn't I ever taught my family what I knew?

The park ranger was silent as we drove through the trees and out of the park. He pulled up in front of a ratty-looking hotel and stopped the vehicle. The paint was peeling, and one window looked boarded up. "You'll still have to make a statement," he said, "but I don't see why that can't wait till you've showered and dried your clothes. The authorities will stop by in about an hour."

I stepped out onto the sidewalk, still in a daze.

"I thought you guys were home-free," said the ranger. "I thought you were the lucky ones."

I nodded and turned toward the front door. Betty and I had gotten lost on the hiking trail at Swan Lake State Park in all the fog and mist and had called for help from our cell phone. We were lost for almost three hours before the park ranger had found us and brought us back to our car. After the ranger got back in his own vehicle, Betty and I had hugged and knelt beside our car to pray.

We'd gone hot air ballooning on our last anniversary. We'd celebrated by skiing our first time the anniversary before that. "Our marriage is an adventure," I told Betty every year, "and we should celebrate an adventure with an adventure."

"Keeping our marriage alive is a constant battle," Betty had replied this year. "Maybe we shouldn't have married in a month named after the god of war."

We finished our prayer of thanksgiving beside the car and then Betty had started to drive us home. She followed what looked like a road but must have been the boat launch. We went right into the water not five minutes after being rescued.

It seemed unnaturally cruel of God.

Or of Heavenly Father, as we were supposed to call him. Betty had always been a stickler for not taking the Lord's name in vain, yet she had yelled out "Oh my god!" over and over at the end. Maybe it didn't count as vain if you were in a life and death situation. But then, since God didn't answer her, it felt as vain as saying it at any other time.

How many times had I gone into our bathroom and closed the door in the middle of the night, getting down on my knees on the cold tile floor and calling out silently, "Oh, God, help me!"

Did God close his eyes when he looked in my direction? I understood why the Greeks and Romans believed in such capricious, dangerous gods.

I opened the hotel door. I had my wallet on me and went up to the desk clerk. "I need a room for the night. We just had an accident at the park."

"I hope everyone's okay," the man said in a dull tone, looking as if it didn't matter to him one way or another.

"Can I get a robe and have you run these clothes through a washer and dryer while I take a shower?" I asked.

"It'll cost you extra." His eyes looked glazed from boredom.

I could see Betty's eyes, pleading with me not to fail her. I wiped my own eyes quickly. "How much?"

We concluded the transaction. I went to my room, put on the robe, and handed my clothes to the clerk, who had followed. I thought briefly about keeping back my garments and drying them myself with a hair dryer, but there were no such amenities in this hotel. I stood in the shower, letting the warm water run down my face and chest.

Betty was dead. A few minutes ago, we'd been joking about how our misadventure would make a great talk in Sacrament meeting. One minute, we'd been heading toward our comfortable, warm home. The next, we were fighting for our lives.

I stayed in the shower for a full twenty-five minutes, but then I thought I'd better make a few phone calls before the police arrived. My clothes weren't ready yet, so I put the bathrobe back on. It was cold and damp from the steam of the shower.

"Destiny," I said into the phone.

"Hi, Dad, what's up?" Destiny was twenty-six and had two children.

"There's been an accident."

I quickly explained what had happened, and then I called Brad and Albert as well. The boys were stunned and speechless, but Destiny had started crying on the phone, making me feel like a murderer. I had barely finished the last call when there was a knock. I opened the door. It was the clerk with my clothes, and two police officers.

I took the clothes and motioned the officers into the room. I made no effort to hide as I pulled on my garments and then my blue jeans and plaid shirt. I put my damp wallet back in my pocket. The officers looked uncomfortable.

"Can you tell us what happened, Mr. Bantam?" one of them asked after I sat down on the bed. They both remained standing.

I shrugged, finding it hard to concentrate. "There's not much to tell. We came out to take a hike on our anniversary. We'd set a goal to lose a little weight a few weeks ago and thought this would be a good way to celebrate our commitment to being the best spouses to each other we could be. We got lost in the fog. We called for help. A while later, the park ranger found us and brought us to our car. Then we drove off right into the lake. I got out but Betty didn't."

"We're going to need more details than that," said the other officer.

Little by little over the next hour, the officers asked the same questions over and over in slightly different ways till they got all the information they wanted out of me. Every answer ended with Betty dead at the bottom of the lake. After saying it a dozen times, I couldn't go on any longer. I put my head in my hands and started crying.

"All right," said one of the officers. "We can finish this in the morning. Don't check out till we've had a chance to talk again."

"I'm not checking out till I find my true love."

The officers looked at each other. "All right, sir. Good night."

After they left, I forced myself over to the door and locked it. Then I sat on the bed again and wondered what kind of life I was going to be able to have without Betty. I was fifty-four, at least fifteen pounds overweight, with salt and pepper hair. My secretary at work flirted with me shamelessly, but I always figured it was because she thought I could buy her things, not because she truly found me attractive.

My parents were still alive, in their eighties, so I likely had a long life ahead of me. How would I ever be able to face it without Betty? She was the only woman I'd ever dated. The only woman I'd ever had sex with. The only woman I could rely on to remain a true friend no matter what secrets I told her. She was my Venus.

Betty had saved my life once when I was about to commit suicide. She'd saved my soul by keeping me a virgin before marriage and monogamous after. She'd collected pressed butterflies with me. She'd baked cookies with me. She'd gone to Berlin with me, and Singapore. She'd read the Book of Mormon with me every night. And I had let her drown.

I'd fought so hard to be worthy of the Celestial Kingdom. Betty and I both had. Was I going to hell now for not saving her? Surely, I could have made more of an effort. I could have held my breath longer if I'd tried a little harder. I could have pulled her out.

Did I *want* to let her drown?

I reached for the phone and made one more call. "Jack? Is that you?" I asked as soon as I heard the phone pick up.

"You okay? You're not canceling on the lesson tomorrow, are you?"

I was in charge of teaching the High Priests Group on Sunday. "Jack, I need a favor."

"Sure, Dennis. Anything.

"Can you come to Swanville, to this hotel called The Waterline?"

There was silence on the other end of the line for a long moment. It dawned on me that I hadn't explained what had happened yet. "Sure. I'll be there in an hour." He hung up before I had a chance to say anything further. What a true friend. Dropping everything and running over, no questions asked.

I lay on the bed as I waited, thinking about Betty, about our three kids, and about their kids. Maybe Betty was lucky, I realized. Her test was over. She'd passed. She'd stayed a good and true and wonderful person till the end. I still had who knew how many years left, filled with the temptation to despair, to work too hard, to work too little, to be too pampering a grandpa, to be too cold.

There would be the temptation to skip church, to stop reading the scriptures, to let myself get even further out of shape, and to satisfy the depraved urges I'd kept repressed now for over forty years.

Why hadn't I saved Betty? She could have helped me overcome all of this, as she'd helped me the last thirty-two years.

Not quite an hour later, there was another knock on my door. I opened it listlessly, and Jack rushed into the room and wrapped me in a tight bear hug. He must have heard something on the news. He started kissing my neck, my ears, my cheeks. Then he started kissing me on the lips. I kissed him back. It seemed the most natural thing in the world to do.

"You don't know how long I've waited for you to call me," Jack said breathlessly. "It's been such a struggle to stay silent. I knew I could never try to come between you and Betty. But if *you* called and asked me to come over, I always knew I'd come."

Jack and I had been friends for fifteen years. Betty and I ate at his house, and Jack and Beth ate at ours. We went to movies together. We went to General Conference together. We played Parcheesi together. We sat at church together. I loved Jack and Betty loved Beth.

"I'm not calling for—" I began. "I'm not—"

Jack looked at me questioningly.

"I'm not…Betty…Jack…"

"What is it, Dennis?" He reached forward and held my hand.

"Betty's dead," I whispered. "She drowned in Swan Lake."

Jack hugged me again. I should feel awful, horrible, I knew, but I'd never felt anything more wonderful in my life. Jack holding me felt so much more loving than any hug Betty had ever given me, yet I knew Betty loved me completely.

Why did Jack's hug feel so different?

We sat on the bed, Jack holding my hand again. "I'm so, so sorry," he said. "I thought you'd called for…"

"I don't know what I'm going to do."

Jack squeezed my hand. "You're going to let me love you," he replied softly. "Not right now, maybe, but soon. I'll be here for you as soon as you're ready." He smiled wanly. "Probably even before you're ready."

I turned to look at him. His eyes were pleading, hungry. I wanted to kiss him again. "You can't leave Beth," I said calmly. It had been such a battle to keep my own marriage alive. I couldn't destroy theirs.

"I've already told Beth that one day I was going to move in with you. She knows. Now that you're almost free—"

"I'm still married to Betty," I said. "We have a temple marriage. We're married for eternity. So are you. You know that."

Jack shook his head. "Heavenly Father is giving us a chance. We need to take it." He closed his eyes. "Not this very minute, Dennis. But soon. It's a gift from Heavenly Father."

"It's not Heavenly Father," I said sadly. "Only Satan would want us to break our vows."

We sat on the side of the bed, Jack scooting over so that he was lying with one of the pillows behind his head. He motioned for me to move over next to him, and I did. "I want to hold you for just a minute," he said. "And then I'll leave." He leaned on one elbow and kissed me again. Then he shifted so that his body was pressed on top of mine. I put my arms around his back.

This was ecstasy.

I pushed him away. "I'm going to the Celestial Kingdom," I said firmly.

Jack looked deep into my eyes, his own showing love and fear and commitment and the deepest sadness I'd ever seen. "I'm quite happy to go to hell for you," he said softly. He put his hand on my chest. I could feel my erection pressing against my pants like a spear.

"Jack…"

"Why did you call me?" he asked. "You had to know how I felt. Why didn't you call someone else? Why didn't you call the bishop?"

He was right. I had slipped. I had sinned. I had hoped for this very thing. And to hear Jack proclaim his love, rather than just subconsciously know it was true, made all the difference in the world. I felt the way I'd felt the first time I put on glasses when I was twelve. Suddenly, the world was clear.

"I love you," I told him. I had wanted so badly finally to be able to say it myself.

Jack reached down into his pocket and pulled something out. He held it out for me. It was a plain silver band.

"Silver?" I asked.

He nodded. "Because I know what we share is Terrestrial rather than Celestial."

I shook my head. "It's not even Telestial," I corrected.

"But it *is*," Jack insisted. "The good, honorable people of the world go to the Terrestrial Kingdom. We're good and honorable."

"We're cheating on our wives."

"Betty's dead," said Jack. "And Beth and I haven't slept together in five years."

"How can you expect me to even think about this just three hours after Betty died?" I pulled my hand away from him, though I was still holding the ring.

"Because I'm selfish and can't bear to wait another minute," he said quietly. "And because you've been thinking about it every day yourself for the past ten years."

My stomach felt hollow. Had I let Betty drown on purpose? Was I hoping we'd get lost on the hiking trail in the first place and Betty wouldn't make it back?

I pulled Jack's face to mine and kissed him again, pulling him on top of me once more. His weight felt glorious. I wanted him more than anything I'd ever wanted. I looked up into his face, and I saw Betty's eyes staring back at me, terrified and pleading. I started to cry.

"It's okay, Dennis," Jack whispered. "It's okay. I love you. I love you."

I pushed him off of me. "I'm moving to Salt Lake," I said. "I have a friend on Mt. Olympus. I can stay with him till I find a job. I need to be around the Saints."

"I'll move, too."

I shook my head. "I want you to leave," I said, enunciating each word carefully, "and I don't want to ever see you again."

"But Dennis…"

"I love you, Jack." I pointed to the door. It was enough that I knew Jack loved me, enough that he knew I loved him. It wasn't an eternity of sex with Betty that I wanted, even if the Celestial Kingdom was the only part of heaven where sex was allowed.

Sex for a billion years couldn't stay interesting, even if it were with Jack. It was the love of a friend that mattered, and Betty had always been a true friend. Perhaps Jack had been as well, but I had to stay true to my wife, my *best* friend.

If she would forgive me on Judgment Day for letting her die.

For killing her.

Jack walked slowly to the door, his shoulders slumped. He paused with his hand on the doorknob, but he didn't look back. After a moment, he opened the door and walked out into the hallway. He closed the door behind him.

I lay in bed, staring at the closed door. Jack would be hoping that in the coming days I would reconsider my position. He'd be praying for me. He'd be waiting for me.

I could still save him, though, keep him married to Beth, give him a chance again at the Celestial Kingdom. Maybe we could both be there.

I breathed out heavily.

I was so tired, so terribly, terribly tired. I stood up and walked to the bathroom, turning on the water to fill the tub, almost to the top. I took off my clothes and folded them on the floor. Then I stepped into the warm water and sat down. The warmth felt like a hug.

I was holding the ring Jack had given me, and now I slid it over my ring finger to rest next to my wedding band.

This wasn't a sin if it was done out of love. I knew it wasn't.

I lay back, letting the water cover my face. Jack, you'll be safe now, I thought. I looked up through the shimmering water at the light in the ceiling, and I saw Betty's face looking down on me. But the face had Jack's eyes.

Then the face of Mars replaced them, looking down on me and smiling. But I smiled back, victorious.

I wasn't willing to drown to save Betty.

I opened my mouth and inhaled.

Killing the Oldest Living Thing

Randilyn sat down in her seat and clicked the seatbelt locked over her lap. She looked out the window to her right, grateful she could see more than just the plane's wing. It would be a peaceful trip back home to Helena from Washington DC, a long time to read the book she'd brought, a long time to look out the window at the landscape below, a long time to reflect and pray and make sure she was right with God after what she'd done.

"Hi," said a man about thirty, with short, dark hair and a single dimple in his left cheek. "I guess we're seatmates, at least to Minneapolis. I'm going on to Helena. What's your final destination?"

The Celestial Kingdom, Randilyn wanted to say. That is, if she repented and got her life back on track. "Helena as well," she said, smiling weakly.

The man's grin widened as he slid into the seat next to her, shoving a small bag under the seat in front of him. "I'm Dwight." He held out his hand.

"Randilyn." She shook it and then looked out the window, wanting to end the conversation. She did not want to talk to a stranger for the next six hours.

"Were you in DC for the inauguration, too?" Dwight asked.

Randilyn felt her face flush but turned back long enough to offer a polite smile. "I went to my niece's wedding."

"In Washington? How fun. Was it in the National Cathedral?"

"The LDS temple," she countered proudly. She might as well try to get some missionary work out of this to make up for her actions the other day.

"Oh, dear."

Randilyn raised an eyebrow. "What do you mean by that?"

"Oh, nothing. Nothing. Are you married yourself?"

She felt her face flush again. There was no way she could put up with this for several more hours. "Very," she said curtly.

"Well, *I* want to be, too, but your church keeps spending millions to prevent it." Randilyn frowned as Dwight struggled to pull out his wallet. He flashed it open to a photo of a man in his late thirties, with sandy blond hair that was thinning a little.

Randilyn didn't mean to recoil, but he was one of *them*. And she'd be trapped here next to him for *hours*. She struggled to look up over the top of the seats in front of her and behind her, but it looked like a full flight. There'd be no way to change seats.

Well, as Relief Society president for the ward, she was looking for a radical topic to give a lesson on next week. This might be just the thing. She had grown bored with the staid, monotonous lessons she and the other sisters gave every Sunday. The Lord worked in mysterious ways. Here she was feeling too sinful to feel the promptings of the Holy Ghost, and Heavenly Father had hand-delivered an answer to one of her prayers.

"Don't you think he's handsome?" Dwight asked, pushing the photo another inch closer to her.

"Not particularly." She didn't want to be mean, but she didn't want to lie, either. Lying was a sin.

Dwight chuckled. "No, I suppose he isn't. I don't love him for his looks. I love him for who he is."

Just then, the flight attendants started their pre-flight instructions and warnings, and Randilyn gladly gave them her attention. As soon as they were done, she looked out the window again. Nothing to see, but she still didn't want to talk. What if Heavenly Father wanted to strike this man down? He must surely be tempted to kill every one of them, what with all the havoc they caused in the world.

Would Dwight be sucked out the window, and Randilyn along with him? Perhaps Heavenly Father would make the whole plane crash. And would the section of plane where this man sat be the area most damaged? She looked over the seat tops again, but the plane was already taxiing.

Even if there had been another seat, she couldn't switch at this point. Soon the runway was flashing past her, so terribly, terribly fast. If anything happened now…

Then they were in the air, and everything was fine.

"So did you get to do anything besides go to the wedding while you were in DC?" Dwight asked casually. "See the Smithsonian? The Newseum? The Library of Congress?"

Randilyn turned and said without emotion, "I spent the time with family. Nothing else is as important as family."

"Oh, I agree. I agree. That's why I want to have one, too."

Randilyn pressed her lips together. It was just like a gay person to try to twist her words around. That's what all liberals did. She felt her face flush again as she remembered how she'd gone to the inauguration parade for Obama's second term, how she'd actually clapped when his car drove by. What had she been thinking?

Naturally, Mormons were by definition patriotic. They loved and supported America in any way they could. But Obama had just beat *Romney*, for goodness' sake. Even if the President had simply been up against any old Republican, it was still clear which party Heavenly Father favored. The Church didn't outright demand that all members be Republicans, but it was obviously the party of the righteous.

Why else would all of the General Authorities and 95% of the members call themselves Republican? The scriptures said that when a majority of the population was corrupt, destruction was soon to follow. Romney had only won 47% of the vote.

It wasn't that you couldn't still be a member in good standing if you were a Democrat, of course. Look at Harry Reid, for example. But there was no doubt a person in the wrong party was on dangerous ground, on the road to apostasy, if they weren't very, very careful. It was simply *easier* to be a sinner if one were a Democrat, and it was the duty of all Latter-day Saints to make sinning as hard as possible, for themselves and for everyone else as well. Romney losing must mean the Second Coming was very near. Randilyn and everyone else needed to repent as quickly as possible.

"I meant real family," she said. "Do you have parents?"

Dwight looked down at his lap. "My mother doesn't talk to me anymore. She says I killed my father. One week after I came out to them, he died of a heart attack. She says he died of a broken heart."

Randilyn almost recoiled again, but even realizing she might be sitting next to a murderer, the story somehow still made her feel just a little bit sorry for her seatmate. What awful knowledge to have to live with, killing one's own father. It was worse than Laman constantly trying to kill Nephi. And it made cheering for the president who might be the devil's representative on Earth seem small in comparison.

Well, maybe not small. Encouraging people who were determined to bring more sin into the world could never be excused. Politics wasn't truly secular like Democrats liked to say. It was very much part of a spiritual war. But at least she hadn't killed anyone.

"My father died hating me. My mother will, too." Dwight was still looking at his lap. "Todd's parents love him. They want us to be happy. But my parents…well, for some people it's more important to follow a stodgy old list of rules than it is to love."

"The Bible isn't a stodgy old list of rules."

Dwight shrugged. "Religious people are always telling gays that you can't pick and choose which parts of the Bible you believe, but aren't they doing the same thing? You don't execute people who miss church on Sunday, do you?"

"What?"

"Your men don't all have beards. You can eat shellfish."

"That's all in the Old Testament."

"As are most of the specific pronouncements against homosexuality."

"But not *all*, right?" Randilyn asked with a tight smile.

"Didn't Jesus say to sell all you have and give to the poor? Do you follow that rule?"

Randilyn sighed. "Look, mister, I don't have the energy for a discussion like this. Can you please just leave me alone?"

A heavyset Hispanic woman bumped into Dwight's seat, presumably on her way to the bathroom. It would have irritated Randilyn, but she noticed that Dwight looked up at the woman and smiled.

"I suppose," he said, turning back toward Randilyn. "It's depressing me, too. But I need some help first, and a mainstream opinion might be just what I need." He dug in his pocket and pulled out a crumpled piece of paper.

Randilyn sent a quick prayer up to heaven to be delivered from this heathen.

"Todd's birthday is Valentine's Day," Dwight said. "I know it's a few weeks off, but I've been struggling with a poem I want to give him. It'll be our first Valentine's Day together. We only met eight months ago."

"You're not going to read me a love poem, are you?" Randilyn asked. "Not a love poem to another man?" She wanted to scoff at the eight months, as if anyone could pretend such a short relationship meant anything. But she didn't want to be mean.

"It'll just take a moment." He smoothed out the paper and began. "Roses are red. Violets are blue. Love someone special. I will choose you."

"Charming." A baby started crying several rows ahead but was silenced after only a few moments.

"It doesn't work?" Dwight looked glum. "I was afraid of that. I want him to be really touched. Here, I have another one."

Randilyn closed her eyes in resignation.

"Roses are red. Violets are blue. I want a man. I think you'll do."

"Oh, for pity's sake."

"Well, I'm a country boy. I don't have the best education in the world. Even educated people aren't always great poets. But this is important. Can I try a few others out on you?"

Randilyn looked at her watch. "Do I have a choice?"

Dwight smiled. "Roses are red. Violets are blue. For Sherlock and Watson, their love is a clue." He looked over at Randilyn. "We love murder mysteries."

"Uh-huh."

"I also like westerns. Every time I try to write a poem for Todd, he calls me a Poet Lariat."

"Maybe you should just buy him a Hallmark card. They screen their card writers pretty thoroughly."

Dwight shook his head firmly. "How about this one?" he asked, smiling eagerly as he looked on his paper for another poem to read. Randilyn couldn't imagine why he was subjecting her to all this when she was clearly not being very supportive. It was just part of his perversity, she supposed. Gays loved flaunting their sin.

"Roses are red. Violets are blue. Love those around you. Good friends are few." Dwight looked at the paper, his head tilting side to side as if balancing on a pivot.

Randilyn frowned. "Nice enough sentiment, but it doesn't sound very romantic." She bit her lip. She hadn't meant to be drawn any further into this conversation. "Oh, look, they're coming down the aisle with snacks."

The next several minutes were spent waiting for their turn to collect a tiny bag of pretzels. Randilyn looked out the window as she slowly ate hers, dragging out the time before the flight attendants made their next round with soft drinks. "I'll have a Coke," said Dwight.

Randilyn couldn't help but let her lip curl a little in disgust. Even though the Church had announced recently that the long-held belief among members that caffeinated drinks were forbidden was not doctrine, Randilyn nevertheless still maintained a bit of judgment over those who drank cola products.

Suddenly, though, she felt like Peter in the New Testament, arguing with God when God said it was okay to eat pork now. Randilyn was part of a living church, after all. They had a prophet who received revelations. To be a good Mormon, one *had* to be willing to accept change.

"I'll have a Sprite," Randilyn told the flight attendant.

When the flight attendant started to reach over Dwight with the cup, her seatmate grabbed it and started passing it on to Randilyn himself. This irked her, but then she cried out when he spilled it right in her lap.

"You did that on purpose!" she hissed.

"I didn't! I was trying to help! I promise!"

The flight attendant handed her several napkins and then another cup, and Randilyn turned as far as she could in her seat toward the window, keeping the cup close to her lips even when she wasn't drinking. She was Relief Society president, she told herself. She had to maintain a certain level of dignity and righteousness.

Heavenly Father had sent this man as a test of her faith. She had to redeem herself. She had to do the right thing. She had to call this man to repentance. So many of these gays were beyond prodigal, beyond hope. But if Heavenly Father had put him in the seat beside her, there had to be a reason.

Randilyn stole a glance over toward Dwight, relieved to see he was reading a book. Good. Maybe she wouldn't have to interact with him again, after all. He was just like her husband, always thinking he was right. Andrew hadn't been able to take a few days off to go with her to Washington. He was important at work, he said. Randilyn had suggested he delegate his duties for just a couple of days, but he wouldn't have it. He didn't *want* to think he was expendable.

So arrogant sometimes. He'd been bishop for four years and first counselor in the stake presidency for another three, but he was bound and determined to rise higher in the Church, and one could only do so if one were successful at business. Randilyn had quoted the prophet David O. McKay when she was buying her ticket to DC. "No other success can compensate for failure in the home."

"Our family isn't a failure just because I don't want to go to your niece's wedding," Andrew had replied. "We haven't seen her more than a dozen times our whole lives. I can't spend *all* my time with family just to prove I'm a good husband and father. I have to earn a living to provide for you, too. That's part of the deal as well, you know."

Whatever.

Randilyn thought again about what she might teach in Relief Society next week. She wanted to talk about temptation and repentance, how repentance didn't just mean being sorry but truly changing in some fundamental way. It was like a mini-baptism, killing one small aspect of your old self at a time and emerging as a new being, little by little, until one achieved perfection. She looked at the man sitting next to her. If she could somehow be the catalyst for getting this man to change, what a great story that would make for her talk.

Dwight closed his book, and Randilyn quickly looked back toward the window. "I can only read so much at a time," he said, yawning. "It's part of my PTSD. It's hard to concentrate as much as I'd like."

"PTSD?" Randilyn couldn't help herself.

"Afghanistan," he replied. "I killed two civilians by accident one day. I was trying to do something good and ended up doing something bad. It's a very difficult thing to live with."

He really *was* a murderer, Randilyn thought, but at the same time, she felt sorry for him again. Why did she keep feeling bad for him just when he told her the most horrific things about himself?

"I'm sorry," she said.

"I was in Afghanistan three years. I saw a lot of terrible things."

Randilyn couldn't help but feel appreciation for this man's bravery and service to his country, though that feeling also sparked a feeling of irritation. "Religious extremists can be so hateful," she sputtered.

"Yes, they can." He looked right at her. Randilyn turned back toward the window.

Randilyn struggled for something else to say. "Well, true religion," she said, "the true gospel, only brings happiness."

Dwight forced a smile. "Tell me the best thing about your life," he said. "What does make you genuinely happy?"

"Well, the Church, of course," she said automatically.

Dwight tilted his head. "The Church truly makes you happier than *anything* else? More than your husband? More than your kids? More than a beautiful sunrise? More than working in a soup kitchen?"

"The Church is like working in a soup kitchen every day," Randilyn replied. "We work almost non-stop helping our fellow brothers and sisters, and that includes our family members."

Dwight nodded. "My church wasn't like that. I guess that's why I don't understand Mormons."

"Would you like to know more about the Church?" Randilyn had managed to get in at least one of the Golden Questions.

Dwight seemed to be thinking, and Randilyn's pulse quickened. "I don't know," he said slowly. "It's just that I don't think any religion could be more important to me than the people I love."

"It's not an either/or proposition. You can have both, love both."

"You can. I can't. And why would I want to leave the man I love, even for God?"

Randilyn gasped. "You—you would put a *person* above *God*?"

"Of course I would."

"You gays have a very distorted view of love."

"I don't mean just my partner. I would put *any* person above God."

Randilyn shook her head. "I don't understand."

Dwight shrugged. "My neighbor won't recycle. He puts everything in one garbage can. It annoys me to no end, but I've talked to him and can't get anywhere. So I accept that this is where he is. When he puts out his trash, I go outside and sort through it and put the recyclables in my own recycle bin. It's a pain in the ass, but this solution is better for my soul than arguing or feeling resentment every day."

"Isn't it illegal to go through someone else's trash?"

Dwight laughed. "I really don't know. But what's right and what's legal aren't always the same thing."

Randilyn gasped again. Then she thought about the federal law banning polygamy back in the nineteenth century which had almost destroyed the Church. She remembered the extermination order in Missouri, where it was legal to kill Mormons for over a hundred years.

"Maybe you have a point," she admitted.

"It's like Todd," he said. "When I tell him it's cold outside, he'll say it's not cold, it's chilly. If I say it's raining, he'll say it's drizzling. If I say it's drizzling, he'll say it's misting. If I say it's hot, he'll say it's warm. It doesn't matter what the issue is. If I say a movie was funny, he'll say no, it was amusing. He contradicts me on absolutely everything."

"Well, that sounds awful. Why would you like such a man?"

Dwight laughed. "It's certainly infuriating at times. But I finally realized it's a compulsion. He has no control over it. He doesn't do it maliciously. He simply can't help himself. I don't know what terrible, deep, dark awful thing happened to him to make him this way. Maybe he was abused and doesn't remember. Maybe some teacher treated him badly back in the second grade. I don't know. I just know I need to accept it as if he had a handicap, because he does."

"Being a jerk isn't a handicap. It's his personality, his spirit, his soul."

"A soul can be handicapped, but that doesn't mean it should be discarded any more than a body that is handicapped should be. I see Todd as if he were blind or deaf. His handicap is hard to live with, just as it's hard for him to live with a man who's lost the bottom half of both legs in Afghanistan." He lifted his right pants leg to show Randilyn a prosthesis.

"Putting up with someone else's handicap is no fun," he continued. "But it isn't any fun being the one *with* the handicap, either, and it isn't fun knowing your disability is making life harder on the one you love." He shrugged. "The least I can do is be accepting."

Randilyn stared at Dwight for the next few moments. Perhaps he wasn't as damaged as she'd first believed. Maybe he was right about handicaps. He might be disabled spiritually, but he wasn't a *bad* man.

"How…how did you meet?" She knew she shouldn't encourage him in any way, but she was curious.

"I was trying to cross the street not long after I got my prostheses. It was taking me longer than it should and the light had already turned. Someone was honking, and that made me flustered and even slower. Todd walked right out into the traffic and helped me to the sidewalk. I was embarrassed and said, 'I'm not a little old lady, you know.' He just laughed and said, 'I'll be *your* old lady if you let me.' How he knew I was gay I don't know. No one in Afghanistan ever guessed. And I've never been that good at figuring out who else might be gay."

He sighed and continued. "One time, I did proposition another guy over there, and he turned out to be very straight." He pointed to his legs. "This was friendly fire, not something the bad guys did."

Randilyn's hand went to her mouth.

"I almost died. I even had one of those near-death experiences you hear about sometimes. When I came back, I knew I absolutely had to live my life to the fullest, no matter what *anyone* else thought."

The fussy baby up front started crying again. Randilyn heard teenage laughter from a few rows behind her. The woman in the seat ahead turned on her overhead light.

Randilyn looked at Dwight's legs and didn't know what to think. Was the man lying, trying to manipulate her? It seemed like the kind of thing a gay man would do.

But he sounded genuine. Just last week, her first counselor had spoken about how they all needed to live lives that had been transformed by an encounter with the divine. Randilyn had *always* been good. There had been no moment of transformation when she suddenly became better than before. "So do you believe in God?" she asked softly.

"Yes," Dwight answered simply. "But I still believe that the best way to honor him is to live a great life, not to tell everybody else how *they* should live."

"But telling other people *helps* them," Randilyn said.

"Not often." He paused. "Have you ever heard of the Prometheus tree?"

She shook her head.

"Back in 1964, there was this grad student out in eastern Nevada taking core samples from bristlecone pine trees. His corer got stuck in one of the trees, and rather than lose it, he cut the tree down. There were lots of trees, after all. Losing one wouldn't hurt anything."

"So?"

"He counted the rings in the tree he cut. It turned out the tree was 4862 years old. Maybe older. It had been cut above the germination point because lower down some of the rings were missing. So it's possible the tree was over 5000 years old. But even at 4862 years, it was the oldest living tree ever discovered. The grad student was out there doing research to help science, and he ended up killing the oldest living thing on the planet."

"Well, that's terrible, but what's your point?" Randilyn sensed Dwight was using some kind of parable, but his audacity at trying to be like Jesus just made her more irritated.

"Lots of people are just plain bad," he said. "But there are lots who try to do the right thing. And even trying to do right, we sometimes do something very bad. We hurt other living things all the time."

"So what's the answer?" asked Randilyn. "Stop trying to do the right thing? How can that help?"

"We'll always make mistakes." Randilyn watched Dwight rub his leg subconsciously. "I think the important thing is not to be so damn sure we're right all the time. Be open to fixing what we've broken. Helping those we've hurt."

Randilyn thought back to the time she'd tried to teach her daughter Margo how to drive. They'd ended up in a ditch, Margo's left shoulder dislocated. Her daughter had missed playing in some important basketball games at school. She blamed Randilyn, though it was clearly Margo who'd been at fault.

Their relationship was still a little strained, even now that Margo was in her first year at BYU. Randilyn wondered if she should apologize, acknowledge Margo's unfair judgment as a spiritual handicap the girl had, accept it and make up for it herself.

Maybe too much time was spent trying to assign blame when the important thing was to fix the problem at hand.

Faith was as old as mankind, starting with Adam and Eve, but cruelty was almost as old, beginning with Cain and Abel. Maybe it was even older, starting with Satan getting Adam and Eve kicked out of the Garden of Eden in the first place. Randilyn was surprised that all this talk with Dwight hadn't shaken her faith, even when she found herself agreeing with him.

"Can I read you another couple of poems?" Dwight asked.

Randilyn smiled wearily. "Just tell him you love him."

"He always holds my hand when I'm going through an episode," he said. "Anything can trigger it, but he always stays there with me till I'm better."

Randilyn nodded, giving Dwight an appraising look.

"I think I'll try reading a few more pages," he said, picking up his book from the seat pocket in front of him.

Randilyn smiled to herself and turned toward the window. "We're descending," she said. "I can make out things on the ground." She stared at the scene below her for a few minutes in silence, not sure if she was glad to almost be rid of her seatmate.

Maybe she'd call Margo from the airport.

"Will you hold my hand when we land?" asked Dwight.

"Yes." Randilyn turned back with a smile for him this time. "Will you eat with me in the airport while we wait for our connection?"

Dwight nodded and smiled in return.

Randilyn looked back out the window. It was growing dark now, and she could see streetlights and house lights down below. She closed her eyes and thought about her Relief Society lesson. She was pretty sure what she would talk about now. Looking downward, she saw car headlights moving ever so slowly along a straight road.

The lights paused at a corner and turned.

The Odds

"The doctor says it's probably genetic," Tom heard his mother say as he watched her pick up her purse and pull a wispy strand of hair away from her forehead. "Of course, the odds of any one child getting it are about 100,000 to 1, so he says your sister's baby will probably be fine."

"That's good," Tom replied automatically.

"Well, we'd better go, dear," his mother said, touching the sofa near his father's knee, but not actually touching him. They stood up and both politely took Tom's left hand briefly before leaving, having spent almost an hour with him here in New Orleans and now ready to head back for their home in Little Rock. They'd be back again in a couple of months for another hour at the crack of dawn. Maybe by then, Tom would be over the shock.

Tom went to the bathroom, averting his eyes as he passed the sink. Not yet, he thought. He couldn't handle it yet.

It was still only 6:30 in the morning, and Tom didn't have to direct his church choir at rehearsal for another twelve hours, so he considered going back to bed. He'd had an easy day yesterday, though, working in the Tulane music library for only five hours, so he really wasn't particularly tired, and he knew he couldn't sleep after what his mom had said. He might dream again.

He took out his music notebook and began composing another anthem. He no longer believed in God, though he'd served two years as a Mormon missionary in Rome. It was there he became engrossed with the Catholic Church, and after resigning from Mormonism a year after his return, he'd started attending Catholic services.

But he'd found his Mormonism conflicted with his new religion, even if he no longer believed. He ended up not believing in any religion at all. Still, he believed in helping the needy, and he'd worked as a volunteer in the Daughters of Charity Catholic healthcare services for a year, which was what brought him to New Orleans in the first place.

Tom's real connection to religion these days was the fact that despite everything, he did love church music. Singing as a tenor and sometimes countertenor each Saturday afternoon for mass at St. Mark's was nice, but it was not much of a challenge. He could sight read too well to get much excitement out of it.

But it was comforting somehow to hear the priest say mass, no matter how much he told himself he didn't believe, and despite the fact it had been three years since he'd taken communion. It made Tom feel exotic to be in a Catholic church, even if Catholics were hundreds of times more common than Mormons. Being one of a billion was better than being one of ten million.

And there was also something comforting about being up in the choir loft away from everyone, behind and above, out of view. People could just think about how good he sounded, without worrying about how he looked.

Maybe that was why he'd been certified as a mobility instructor to teach blind students how to get about the city by themselves. He'd started college just before his seventeenth birthday and completed simultaneous degrees in music and psychology before he was twenty, only then going on his mission. He hadn't been sure he'd go at all at first.

His bishop had said diplomatically, "Perhaps your mission is in music, like the Osmonds." But Tom wanted to be just like everyone else, at least for two years, at least in one respect, and he was deeply grateful he had gone. Rome had changed his life. It had started him down the road to spiritual liberation. Only one out of a hundred ever freed themselves from the bonds of religion, and he was happy to be one of them.

After returning to the U.S., he thought again about work. He realized there would be few job opportunities in either music or psychology, so he'd gone on to get a Masters in Special Education. Everyone had urged him to work with the physically disabled or as a musical therapist, but Tom had wanted something totally apart from himself.

After teaching mobility for two years in Jackson, Mississippi, and being fired for speaking publicly about being gay, he'd moved to New Orleans, worked with mentally disabled adults through the Daughters of Charity, and finally decided he needed something more "normal."

It was then, at the age of twenty-six, when he'd really come out. Of course, he'd known since he was ten that he was gay and had never felt the least bit guilty. It was simply a part of him. But it was just a few months later, as he tried to bring up the subject with some friends, only to find them totally disgusted with him, that he'd finally realized what society really felt towards gays.

"Oh, God," Tom had prayed. "This too? Having one arm wasn't enough?" Only one person in ten was gay. Why did it have to be him? It wasn't fair.

Maybe that was why he couldn't believe any more. Or maybe it was listening to the fundamentalists condemn him on TV. Or listening to the fundamentalists condemn each other. Or watching "Christians" carry a huge cross through the French Quarter on Mardi Gras. Or maybe it was wondering how the Church could tell him his mother shouldn't have had an abortion twenty-eight years ago.

David still believed, though. Tom looked at his watch, hanging loosely on his thin wrist. He was grateful his hand was at least big enough to keep his boyfriend's gift from sliding off completely. 6:45. David was probably up, but Tom didn't want to disturb him yet. He wished David were here so he could know whether he was busy, and Tom wondered if David would ever give in about living together.

Tom looked about the apartment, seeing the clothes strewn everywhere, trash flowing out of a bag that hadn't been emptied in a month, and a dirty spoon on the floor next to his open *Honcho*. He groaned, wishing he'd seen the magazine in time to put it away.

Of course, his mother knew, and she was probably glad he got some kind of sexual satisfaction, since Tom never told her about David. He'd certainly never told her about the hustlers he'd bought twice a month for two years before he met David, and the one, single gorgeous hustler he still enjoyed once a month, even though he'd been with David for over a year now.

David knew about the hustler and said he didn't care, which Tom found hard to believe. David also knew that Tom had slept with three other guys over the past year, and insisted he didn't care about that, either. Tom wondered if that meant David didn't really want to be his lover, but he and David had sex three nights a week.

They took showers together, ate together if David could make sure his plate and glass were clean first, and they even played games together sometimes, *Dark Shadows* once after they'd reminisced about the old TV show, or Trivial Pursuit or Boggle or whatever.

They also took walks together through the Quarter, David having learned how to hold Tom's left hand though only two of his four fingers worked and none of them had joints, two of them also sticking out at such odd angles that most people who started to shake his hand usually ended up shaking his wrist instead.

And they'd see dollar movies together, watch *The Golden Girls* while eating butter pecan ice cream, read medieval history books together, go grocery shopping sometimes, and just talk. David said that being best friends meant they were lovers, but Tom wanted them to live together. David would point to a moldy cup on the table or to the roaches scampering across the floor or sofa and shake his head.

"I don't think I can ever live with you," he'd say. "Can't we be lovers and just live down the street from each other?"

Tom had stopped being offended at the remark. David didn't understand that Tom had never once had to clean up for himself. His mother had always done it for him. It wasn't as if Tom was incapable of it, of course. He could shop for himself and cook for himself. He could even play the organ using his two good fingers on this left hand and the two stubs coming out of his right shoulder. Those, at least, had one joint each.

He didn't clean, though, because he simply didn't care. David had asked if maybe he wanted people to be turned off by his apartment so that he could say it was his apartment and not his body that kept him from having more friends. David would get particularly upset when Tom would spill food on his clothes, asking if Tom couldn't at least wear one outfit to eat and get dirty in and keep the rest clean.

He did do his laundry every three weeks now instead of every six, and he had finally gotten around to cleaning the stove, but to keep his place as clean as David's apartment? People had turned away from his deformed arms and his slight hunchback for years. Why should he go to so much trouble when he knew people would still turn away?

Of course, David hadn't turned away. They'd met at a party after the Gay Men's Chorus Christmas concert, where Tom had sung a countertenor solo. Tom had learned how to be aggressive in his two years in the bars, and how to go on to the next attack when turned down, so he'd headed for the young, muscular blond with only moderate fear.

But David hadn't turned him down. They'd talked for three hours, about music (George Michael versus Bach), the latest movies, a book Tom had just read on the Pol Pot regime and one David had just read by Florence King. They talked about judging things on the surface, since David had just come out six months before and was being judged by almost everyone he'd ever known.

They talked about David teaching first grade, trying to reach "that one person out of thirty," about Tom writing a one-act play and his brief career as an actor in three plays (as a disabled child, a mentally disabled adult, and a burn victim), and they simply talked about *everything*.

Tom looked at his watch again. Maybe he should call David, after all. He'd understand why he needed to talk. He'd been the only one who understood why Tom had wanted to quit teaching mobility and try to make a living with his music, even though he'd make less money.

He understood how applying as choir director at a suburban Presbyterian church had been an act of almost unbelievable courage for Tom, choosing deliberately to stand in front of an entire congregation and be the single focus of attention for a hundred people every time he stood up.

Yes, he could tell David. David was the only one he'd ever dared tell about the hustler. And he was the only one who ever just listened to his dreams about being aborted without trying to tell him what they meant. David would understand. As much as anyone else could, anyway, who hadn't had to go through it. David would accept his self-pity, too, if he asked why if he'd had to beat such odds, he couldn't have won the lottery instead.

Funny how all these years, he'd figured his condition was the result of nuclear testing or the side effect to a drug.

He thought he'd accepted it a long time ago, but something about hearing his mother tell him it was probably genetic made him want to scream, made him want to hit his mother, hit the doctor, hit his father and his sister.

Why *me*? It was such a stupid question. Everyone who ever broke a toe or lost a dog or ended an affair thought the same thing. And the blind students he'd worked with had asked the question, and the parents of the mentally disabled adults had asked it. Even his own parents had undoubtedly asked it.

Tom picked up the phone and dialed. Fourteen months with David and they still got along. When they slept together, they cuddled all night long, one of them always draping an arm across the other, Tom sometimes sleeping with his head on David's shoulder, both of David's arms wrapped around him.

Maybe there was a God.

"Hello?"

"David? It's Tom."

"Hey, sweet thing. What're you doing up so early?"

"I didn't wake you, did I?"

"No. I'm finishing some plans for class."

"My parents just left," Tom told him. "I need to talk about it. Do you have a little time before you go to the school?"

"Sure. Be over in a few minutes."

They hung up, and Tom wiped off the table, putting the dirty dishes in the sink, and making sure to pick the spoon off the floor. He washed the dishes twice a week now, and he'd finally mopped the bathroom floor the other day. Only one person in a dozen ever managed to overcome deeply ingrained bad habits. But he was getting there. And David was patient.

He said Tom was a dream come true for him, and that he loved Tom more every day. What were the odds in finding a love like that? Maybe one day he and David really could live together. Maybe David would move in on their fifth anniversary. Or their tenth. Or maybe on their second.

He smiled and poured some soap in the sink.

Bumper Sticker Theology

"Are you sure you won't come?" Henry asked. "You can go as you are. It's casual." At forty-three, Elizabeth could still look stunning when she wanted to. And he certainly didn't want to go today looking like a single forty-five-year-old man. He stood at the door with one hand on the knob, afraid to open it.

"No," Elizabeth said coldly. "And I'm still debating whether or not to call the bishop."

"Oh, Elizabeth, you know I have no choice."

"There's always a choice between sinning and not sinning."

"I have no choice!" Henry opened the door, quickly walked through it, and shut it behind him firmly. Mormon wives were supposed to support their husbands, he thought angrily. He was the breadwinner in the family, after all. Elizabeth shouldn't be so hard-nosed.

He sat behind the wheel in his PT Cruiser. The car had been so hip when it first came out, but then the market had become glutted, and the manufacturer never did come out with any daring new models. Just the one. Henry, though, had bought the vehicle before everyone jumped on the bandwagon. *He* was adventurous.

Henry grumbled as he pulled away from the house. Driving from Fremont in north Seattle up to Mukilteo was such a pain. Chase and Jordan lived reasonably nearby in Seward Park. There was no reason the ceremony had to be held way up on Whidbey Island. It was just like gay people to make life difficult for everyone around them.

Chase was Henry's boss at Costco, heading one of the HR divisions. He was nice enough, but he had his own way of looking at things, and heaven forbid anyone thought differently.

To be honest, Henry usually agreed with him on most things, but he could never shake the feeling that he was just a yes man, going along with everything because he was afraid of losing his job. Chase hadn't specifically ordered Henry to attend his wedding, but three other people from the department were going, and Henry felt it was better to be safe than sorry.

Traffic was thick and slow, lots of people trying to get away from the city for the weekend. It was the first week of July, around 68 degrees, without a cloud in the sky. Perfect weather for an outing.

Damn Elizabeth for making this even harder than it had to be.

An SUV passed by in the lane to his right. Henry noticed the bumper sticker on the rear of the vehicle. "One man, one woman. As God intended. Vote no on Ref. 74." Henry groaned. He had a similar bumper sticker on the back of his own car. He'd tried to peel it off a couple of days ago to be ready for today, but the infernal thing was stuck permanently.

If only the citizens of Seattle weren't overly ripe for destruction, they'd have voted against the referendum.

In his rearview mirror, Henry could see Mt. Rainier towering above everything, its top half so high that even in the middle of summer it was still covered in snow. And ahead and to the right, he could see Mt. Baker, also covered in snow. Heavenly Father would surely make one of the volcanoes erupt before long, or cause another big earthquake, or a tsunami, or *something*. This much wickedness couldn't go unchecked forever.

After almost an hour, Henry arrived in Mukilteo. He didn't get in the line for the ferry but drove straight to the parking area. He was going on as a foot passenger. Chase had offered the option of being chauffeured in a van from the ferry station on the other side, and Henry had jumped at the chance. It took fifteen minutes to find a parking space, and just as Henry bought his $4.65 ticket, he heard the gate closing. He'd just missed the ferry. Thirty minutes now until the next one.

Perhaps that was Heavenly Father giving him another chance to back out. There were supposed to be fifty people at the wedding. Chase wouldn't miss him. Henry could come up with some excuse.

Liars went to the Telestial Kingdom, the lowest degree of heaven.

Henry was going to the Celestial Kingdom, the highest degree. Only those with a temple marriage could go there. There was talk that good people who'd never found a lifemate could also reach the Celestial Kingdom, but Henry wasn't sure those folks wouldn't instead be relegated to ministering angel status rather than godhood like he and Elizabeth.

All this talk of legalizing same-sex marriage was ridiculous. Nothing outside of the temple mattered anyway. Not even regular heterosexual marriages performed in city halls or churches or synagogues counted. Heavenly Father was quite explicit on the subject.

Chase was Jewish. What chance did he have in any event? And Jordan was an atheist. It was laughable that Henry was afraid of losing his job when these men had lost both salvation and exaltation.

Three gay men appeared near the gate, waiting for the next ferry as well. They looked enough like real men, Henry supposed, but he could just *tell*. Something about the way they joked and laughed. They seemed too happy, the way only people who had no thought for the consequences of their actions could.

Just before 3:00, Henry looked up and saw the ferry approaching. The water churned heavily as it came to a stop. Workers tied ropes and let down a ramp. Then about twenty people walked off, followed by a horde of vehicles. Henry walked on next, trailing behind the gay men.

There was also an obese woman laughing with them now. Henry had heard that lesbians were fat. This woman looked straight, though, probably just friendless because of her weight and willing to accept anyone who talked to her.

Henry climbed two flights of stairs and headed to the front of the ferry, where there was a tiny landing surrounded by a guard rail. As the ferry started out across the water, Henry luxuriated in the feel of the strong breeze against his face. His shirt was billowing in the wind, and the temperature out here felt at least ten degrees cooler than it had on land. He looked at the tiny whitecaps on the water and the island rising majestically out of the Sound ahead of him. Such beauty. The Celestial Kingdom must be something like this.

Chase and Jordan had better enjoy it while they could.

Henry watched as the houses along the shore of Whidbey Island grew larger. He always enjoyed ferry rides. He'd gone to Vashon and Bainbridge and even up to Victoria in British Columbia with Elizabeth and the two boys. It was always fun.

He grinned now, remembering a song he and his friends used to sing on the school bus on the way to middle school. The bus driver was named Mrs. Jolly, and her son rode the bus, too. Henry and the others used to sing every day, "Hooray for the bus driver, the bus driver, the bus driver. Hooray for the bus driver, the bus driver, hooray. She's Jolly, she's merry, her kid is a fairy. Hooray for the bus driver, the bus driver, the bus driver. Hooray for the bus driver, the bus driver, hooray."

Henry wondered whatever became of that kid.

Probably died of AIDS years ago.

Henry used to wonder why the bus driver had allowed them to keep singing that song. He finally realized it was probably because she felt it would knock the boy back in line. She allowed those lyrics every day because she loved her son.

You always had to make it clear to gay people that you didn't accept their choices in life. It was the only way to help them.

Was Henry selling his soul by attending this wedding?

Once on the island, Henry followed the small group, hoping they knew where the van was waiting. The three men and one woman had been joined now by another woman, young and pretty, clearly straight. Henry didn't recognize her from work, but perhaps she was a friend of Jordan's.

Jordan worked in technical writing at Costco, so Henry rarely saw him there. The group walked toward a red van, and when Henry drew close enough, he could see a sign reading "Chase" against the windshield. He hurried and joined the others as they were climbing into the van.

"Hi," said one of the gay men as Henry sat next to him. The man offered his hand. Henry shook it unhappily. "I'm Joey."

"Henry."

Everyone else introduced themselves. Henry felt more and more tainted as the van drove on. He tried to focus on the scenery, the winding roads, the fir trees with their branches turning the roads into tunnels. After a few miles, the driver veered onto a gray gravel road, and the branches formed an even darker canopy.

Soon they were so deep into the wildnerness that the road had grass growing between the wheel ruts. Henry worried for a moment if this was all a trick of some kind, a kidnapping to get innocent people deep into the woods to rape them.

Eventually, they pulled up to a bland looking house, really just a double-wide mobile home with siding added. There was also a huge garage almost as big as the house. Lots of people were milling about. Henry wished Elizabeth were here.

She was home helping Steven practice his going away talk. Their eighteen-year-old had been called to serve a mission in Quebec and would be leaving in a few weeks. He'd be giving his talk not tomorrow, which was Fast and Testimony day, but the following Sunday. Elizabeth wanted to make sure he did a good job. She was being the real parent this weekend, while Henry was just being a good employee.

What had President David O. McKay said? No other success can compensate for failure in the home.

Well, the boy was going on a mission, wasn't he? Henry hadn't done too bad a job. And Dane was still attending Seminary classes and preparing for his turn in two more years.

Dane was a worry, though. Even though he was sixteen and old enough to date, he'd never asked a single girl out. He seemed masculine enough, however. He played basketball at church, soccer at the school, and liked math. Surely, there was nothing wrong with him. He always laughed when Henry recounted his story of singing on the school bus as a child.

Or when he told Steven and Dane about the time he and some other boys pulled the pants down on a boy in their ninth-grade gym class. They were in the locker room, and the boy always looked at Henry when he was changing clothes, so he'd finally gotten his friends to help. They'd pulled Randy's pants down around his ankles, and then every one of the seven other boys had hit Randy in the balls, leaving him writhing on the ground when they were finished.

The boy never came back to school again.

Henry frowned. Well, it wasn't all that different from what Mitt Romney had done, was it?

You had to be firm with gays. They thought they deserved the world. You had to teach them their place. Otherwise, it was like letting Lance Armstrong get away with doping. No one would stop speeding if the police never issued any tickets. Unless you made it clear something was unacceptable, people were just going to keep doing it.

Was it too late to take the van back to the ferry terminal? It was too far to walk, and Henry couldn't remember the way in any event.

He was stuck.

"Please, Heavenly Father, please make this wedding go poorly," Henry prayed silently. "Please teach them a lesson."

There were several cars parked in the driveway. As Henry passed them on his way to the back yard, he read a bumper sticker on a blue hybrid. "Love ALL families." Henry groaned. He walked past the first table beside the garage, filled with Costco vodka and Costco wine. There were also two dozen beer bottles. A huge glass container looked to be filled with sliced lemons in ice water. And there were six large bottles of Perrier water.

On a table next to the beverages were a few platters with food: toasted slices of a tiny bread, each slice the size of an old-fashioned silver dollar; chunks of various cheeses with cheese knives next to them; olives and cherries; and tiny skewers with two grape tomatoes surrounding a tiny mozzarella ball on each one.

But the best thing of all was the flies. They were *everywhere*. Flies on the food. Flies on the drinks. Flies on the faces of all the people. Everyone was waving away flies non-stop.

God had sent a plague. How wonderful! God understood. God was going to do the right thing even if Henry was weak. Henry knew he had a good story for tomorrow's Fast and Testimony meeting at church. He felt the Holy Spirit testifying to him.

Henry made his way to Chase, who was petting a mongrel dog. "Congratulations on your special day," Henry said, shaking Chase's hand.

"Thank you for coming." Chase swiped at a fly.

Henry stood off to the side and observed everyone else for a few moments. Chase introduced some people to his mother, an ancient woman who looked very frail. Chase couldn't be any older than Henry, so it was surprising to see such an old woman. Chase must have been her baby. Spoiled, no doubt. That certainly helped explain the homosexuality.

And Jordan was introducing people to his mother, an attractive woman probably around sixty but looking younger. Jordan was probably around thirty-five. He had a slightly

British accent, but Henry always figured the man was just affected.

Jordan saw him looking in his direction and waved him over. Henry decided he might as well play his part if he was going to be there. He shook Jordan's mother's hand, noting with surprise that she had an accent, too. "Where are you from?" he asked.

"Capetown," the woman replied. "I'm so happy I could make it for Jordan and Chase's wedding. And Enid came up from Los Angeles in the middle of her chemotherapy. She didn't want to miss this." She nodded in the direction of Chase's mother.

Henry was dumbfounded. These guys had invited their parents? And they'd actually come? Well, there were clearly no fathers about. Henry supposed they might be dead, but it seemed just as likely these overindulgent mothers had come alone.

There were three large plastic tables set up with six or seven chairs around each one. They were covered by large tents. Elsewhere on the lawn, people lounged on several red and white plaid blankets. Henry took a walk around the property by himself to avoid having to talk too much. He noticed, of course, the thick woods all about, huge trees maybe two or three feet apart, the property almost too thickly wooded to walk.

Only the immediate yard was cleared of trees, and even here, there were three fig trees and a crabapple tree. Tiki torches burned at intervals, but they clearly weren't scaring away any of the insects. In front of the house was a green hammock, the rear wheels and rusted axle of a wagon, a pair of antlers propped on a box, and several trees covered in silk caterpillar webs, repulsive.

A heterosexual couple was walking along with their three-year-old daughter. Teaching the child at this impressionable age that gay weddings were normal. Henry made his way back to the rear of the house and hoped the ceremony would begin soon. He looked at his watch and gritted his teeth.

A server came around with a tray and offered Henry a doughy object. "It's phyllo dough with brie and sliced pears. Careful. They're hot." Henry took one and bit carefully into it, waving at his mouth with his hand. He was supposed to be fasting, but he had to try to fit in.

"Good, aren't they?" said a woman near him. She had a tattoo. Henry wondered if she was a lesbian.

Henry nodded and moved to a table where there was an empty seat. It looked like all the tables with normal heterosexuals were already filled. These people all pretended to be so tolerant, Henry sneered, but the gays were still all sitting by themselves. Such liberal hypocrites. Henry didn't feel like sitting on the grass, so he took a deep breath and went to the gay table. He waved a fly from his face.

The men next to him at the table were talking and laughing. Henry tried to ignore them, but part of their conversation caught his ear. "I was in southern Italy for New Year's," said one man with a slightly bushy beard. "I think that's where the saying, 'Out with the old, in with the new,' comes from. Everyone throws out their old furniture from their windows. People have to park their cars off the street to protect them."

"When I lived in San Francisco," said another man, clean-shaven but heavily muscled, "the people there threw out old calendars on New Year's Eve. Of course, in the Castro, they threw out Colt calendars. I used to pick them up and save them."

Everyone laughed. Henry wasn't sure what they were talking about. Probably something about bestiality and gay men.

He sure wished Elizabeth had come, if for no other reason than they'd have something to talk about later. They had so little to talk about these days. Steve and Dane. And what the bishop had said during Sacrament meeting.

Well, that was plenty.

Henry tried to ignore the flies and the talk, and about forty-five minutes later, a fat woman sat on a chair in a little clearing and started playing a harp. Then a well-dressed woman around thirty stood in front of a fig tree covered in Chinese lanterns, holding a book.

Two women, one a knockout with deep auburn hair and a hunter green dress, walked up and stood to one side of the lady holding the book, and two men in dark suits walked up and stood to her other side. Then Chase walked out slowly, holding his mother's arm, followed by Jordan, holding his mother's arm.

The two mothers sat down at a table, and all the others in the wedding party stood in front of the fig tree. The lady with the book started speaking, "We gather here today to witness the union of two people who love each other."

Henry managed not to groan loudly enough to be overheard. The woman made a few more remarks and then said, "And now I'd like to read Pablo Neruda's Sonnet 17."

She did read it, and it was lovely enough, but it didn't compare to looking at an infinity of mirrors pointing toward each other in the temple as one knelt at a padded altar in front of a man who held the keys to eternity. It was sad, really, to watch these ignorant people who thought they had something special when they truly only had an inferior brand of love.

The worst part was that they didn't even realize it. It was like watching a poor beggar eat a slice of stale Safeway bread, having no concept that he could have a slice of rich Rosemary Diamante bread from QFC instead. It was like someone eating a Little Debbie raisin pie when he could have a slice of The Cheesecake Factory's pumpkin cheesecake. It was like eating a can of Spaghetti-O's instead of lasagna from Il Fornaio.

It wasn't like these people were eating *dirt*, of course. What they were eating was edible enough. It just wasn't the delicacy he and Elizabeth were used to. And Henry knew both Chase and Jordan well enough to be quite aware their love was far from perfect. They complained about each other all the time.

Henry had been coerced to go to a couple of parties at their home in Seward Park. Chase was always bemoaning Jordan's moodiness, and Henry had heard Jordan a time or two talk about Chase's insensitivity.

But here they were, trying to make a political statement that their love was equal to anyone else's.

They were only kidding themselves.

The woman with the book was still talking. "Chase and Jordan met over fourteen years ago in London at a 'gentlemen's club.'"

Everyone laughed. Did that mean "bar"? What was so funny?

"And they've worked hard to build a relationship ever since. Jordan has had to go back to South Africa twice because of visa issues, but now with the Supreme Court ruling on DOMA, the United States will officially recognize Chase and Jordan's marriage, and Jordan can finally get a green card."

Special rights. That's all gays seemed to be after. Henry tried to keep a blank face as the ceremony continued. He waved away a fly. Soon the woman with the book was having each of the grooms repeat their vows, and then the two men kissed.

Henry had been prepared for it, so he didn't flinch.

And that was it. They were done. Henry breathed a sigh of relief and wondered when the van would start carrying people back to the ferry terminal. A long-haired man, a frumpy woman, and another man with wild white hair started playing music, a slow song, and Chase and Jordan danced while everyone cheered.

Henry wondered if he could sneak another of those phyllo dough things from the catering table. Near the end of the song, Chase asked the crowd to join in the dance, and about ten couples complied, almost three quarters of them heterosexual couples. Why were so many heterosexuals celebrating a gay wedding? It just didn't make sense.

There was no van. The little girl chased the mongrel dog. Chase and Jordan danced some more. And the band kept playing, a few French songs now. Then one of the men who'd been in a suit during the wedding took the microphone away from the long-haired man and sang the old 1970's classic, "If," by Bread.

He did a decent job of it, even if his mannerisms were a little effeminate. Then he returned the mike back to the bandleader, but before the long-haired man could start singing again, Chase waved at the audience.

"You might have noticed all the picnic baskets as you came in," he began. "Each one has someone's name on it, and they each have plates, cups, and utensils inside. They're our gift to you for sharing with us your gift of love. Go pick up your baskets, and the caterers are bringing out dinner right now."

Henry had wondered about the baskets when he first arrived. He waited for the crowd to die down and then walked over. Sure enough, there was a wicker picnic basket with his name on a card. The gesture touched him, but then he remembered that Costco had put these baskets on sale about a month ago.

He picked up his basket, waited in line at the food table, and grabbed an eggplant sandwich on French bread, a salad, and a slice of pineapple sprinkled with a touch of cinnamon.

He sat back at his table, swatted at a couple of flies, and began eating.

Henry looked at his food, and the others at the table seemed to understand that he didn't want to talk and didn't try to engage him. The only problem was that he could still hear them. One woman talked about how she had marched in the Gay Pride parade the year before as part of the Catholics for Marriage Equality contingent.

But then, Henry had always known that the Catholic Church was the whore of Babylon. Then, after about twenty or thirty minutes of irritating political comments, four of the men at the table started talking about how they met.

"Jeff and I met in the bushes at Volunteer Park," said the man with the slightly bushy beard.

"Do you remember the date?" asked one of the other men, slim, with a tattoo of barbed wire on his upper arm.

The first man laughed. "Of course. That's our anniversary."

"Our first date was a little more conventional," said the other man with the barbed wire tattoo. "We met in the back room of the Eagle. That's the date we celebrate, too."

This was true love? Henry had taken just about as much as he could bear of all this. The flies were in *his* face, too, because he was sinning as much as anyone else by being here. What should he do, he wondered. What would Joseph Smith do in his place?

"We've been together twelve years."

"Seventeen for us."

Henry felt his face flush. This was intolerable. Joseph Smith would testify, that's what he'd do. So would Parley P. Pratt. They never bothered to fear for their safety. The truth was what was important to them because that was what was important to God.

Abinadi spoke the truth without worrying about the consequences. So did Nephi.

If Elizabeth did report him to the bishop, Henry could say he'd borne his testimony to the crowd, that he talked of true marriage, that he'd stood up for what was right when he might be the solitary righteous person in attendance.

But he might also by his courage bring down the Holy Ghost upon the crowd, like Ammon did for King Lamoni. Dozens of people might be brought to repentance and end up being baptized.

Henry just needed to be strong and brave.

Henry stood and moved purposefully away from the table. He walked past the food trays and headed toward the band. They were taking a break, and the microphone was standing unattended. He could do this. He could really do this.

Elizabeth would stop being so negative all the time.

It would put Steven in the right spirit for his mission.

It would cure whatever might be Dane's problem.

And Henry would have a *great* story to tell in Fast and Testimony meeting.

This might even be the one act he needed to have his calling and election made sure. It would take a lot of guts, but Henry already had a temple recommend. It meant he was already doing all of the "normal" good things he was supposed to be doing. Lots of them.

But this would be a *great* thing.

So what if he lost his job? So what if people laughed? He wasn't going to be like those weaklings in Lehi's dream who let go of the iron rod because people in the great and spacious building were jeering at them.

Henry felt downright filthy at this God-forsaken gay wedding. He needed to cleanse himself. He was going to turn this obstacle into a steppingstone.

He picked the microphone out of its stand and held it to his lips.

His legs were trembling.

He was a great man.

Henry could see several people looking at him curiously. Even Chase and Jordan were looking his way. His heart was pounding. He cleared his throat.

"I just want to wish the happy couple another wonderful fourteen years," said Henry. "And another fourteen after that."

People clapped politely, and Henry hurried to the beverage table and grabbed a cup of lemon water. As he was gulping it down hurriedly, spilling half on his shirt, he saw the red van pull up out front. He dropped his cup on the ground and almost ran to be first getting in.

The guys who'd had sex with horses in San Francisco slid into the van after him, one of them pressing his leg against Henry's. A straight couple also pushed their way in. Henry ignored the chatter between the others and stared out the window till they were at the terminal. Then he lagged behind so he could wait for the ferry apart from the small group.

When the ferry finally came, about fifteen people walked off, followed by some motorcycles and a bevy of cars. One had a bumper sticker that read, "Coexist," made up of various religious symbols. It barely registered in the back of Henry's mind.

He walked aboard with determination and stood at the railing on top, clutching it tightly. Soon the breeze picked up, and he watched the whitecaps as Mukilteo slowly approached across the Sound. Henry looked at Mt. Baker in the distance, then at Mt. Rainier.

Gay people were so wicked, he thought bitterly. So self-indulgent and weak. They brought everyone down around them.

Henry waved at something in front of his eyes, though he couldn't see just what it was.

He thought about what he might say in Fast and Testimony meeting tomorrow. He was going to give a good talk. Elizabeth and the boys would be proud.

Henry brushed in irritation again at his face, though there were no flies anywhere about.

A Grain of Mustard Seed

"John, you need to take a fourth wife," Bishop Hughes said, smiling cordially. "I'd suggest either Helen Halvorson or Isabel Thomas. But you pray about it and ask one of the women in the ward by next Sunday."

John was dismayed. Having three wives already and nine children was almost more than he could bear. When would the Lord stop testing him?

"All you need is faith the size of a mustard seed," the bishop said, "and you can do anything."

John forced a smile. Hadn't it been enough, though, that John and his first wife, Elaine, had left England for America, leaving behind their families and all their worldly possessions so they could join the saints in Nauvoo? Hadn't it been enough to then serve a mission himself, leaving behind his wife and young son for an entire year, only to be tarred and feathered?

His left arm was permanently scarred from the ordeal. And hadn't it then been the final test to leave behind his worldly goods a second time and walk across the plains on foot to join the prophet in Salt Lake City, in the middle of a desert? What more could God want?

"Yes, Bishop, I'll pray about it. And ask my other wives what they think."

"Oh, of course, of course." The bishop smiled. "Never hurts to ask the women what they feel." He chuckled.

John walked home slowly. He again regretted having the surname Smith. Not every man was called to plural marriage, but with that name, everyone thought he was related to Joseph, and he had to set an example. He'd been quite upset to be commanded to marry Mary Dickinson not long after reaching the Valley. Did the bishop truly know what he was talking about?

Part of John had liked the idea, of course. He'd never felt particularly close to Elaine, and while intimidated to be with a second woman, he was nevertheless curious to know if this relationship would work out better than the first.

It didn't. Mary was pleasant enough, and Mary and Elaine got along well, but somehow the presence of a second woman in the house simply made John feel even more alone than before.

Some men set up separate households for their different wives. But John couldn't afford that, and he felt that at the very least, the two wives could be friends and support each other.

That second marriage had only been in effect two years when the bishop called John to take a third wife, Elizabeth, and now, not even three years after that, he was being ordered to take a fourth. When would it all end? Surely, he wouldn't wind up like Brigham himself? John tried to hold onto the tiny hope that he was finally about to make his calling and election sure.

He trudged home slowly, and as soon as he entered the door, Elizabeth said, "I think we're getting another sister."

John explained what the bishop had said, and Elaine offered cautiously, "Well, I think Isabel is the better cook."

"But Helen has a sweeter personality," Mary countered.

"We should invite Isabel over for lunch on Tuesday," said Elizabeth, "and have Helen over on Thursday."

John nodded. "Can you girls let me know by Saturday?"

Elizabeth laughed. "Don't you want to have a say in this?"

"It's more important for you three to feel comfortable."

"You didn't marry me because you loved me?" continued Elizabeth, laughing. "You let your other wives choose me?"

John didn't answer, and Elizabeth's smile faded as she stole a quick glance at her sisters.

There was no truly private place in the house, but John wanted to be alone, so he ignored the children clamoring for attention and went to his primary bedroom, the one he shared with Elaine, and closed the door. Little Samuel was asleep in his crib, but this was as private a place as he could find, so John kneeled on the floor beside the bed.

"You can transform water into wine," he said. "You can move mountains. You can turn two fishes into a feast for thousands. You have complete power over material nature. Please, please, can you turn me into what I so long to be?"

He waited on his knees, his head bent, but he felt nothing change in his body. He reached up to feel his chest, but there were still no breasts. He reached down to his crotch, but he could still feel his member filling his pants.

A tear began to form but he shook it aside.

John wasn't sure he really wished to be a woman. He remembered a time when he was twelve and had put on his sister's dress, just for laughs, and his father had beat him. His father then forced him to spend thirty minutes with a streetwalker to "purify" him. John had been compelled to perform with his father looking on.

The shame he felt was so great that he could only feel the tiniest kernel of goodness still in him. Years later, when he heard the elders on the street corner preaching, he immediately knew he could find forgiveness and peace among the Mormons.

He'd been completely faithful to Elaine, and then later to all his wives. He had set times to be with each, and he always attended to them with steadfastness and kindness. Once, Mary had been feeling lonely and asked for a special visit, but it had been Elizabeth's night and he declined. Mary later told him he'd made the right decision, that the only way the household could manage was if no one wife tried to usurp another.

The truth was that John's wives were all very close to each other, and this pleased John very much. Yet despite that, he felt no real kinship with them at all. If he were truly to be a woman like them, wouldn't he at least feel sisterly toward them?

All he knew was that he wanted to be the wife of Bishop Hughes, and to do that, he'd have to be a woman himself. Bishop Hughes had been there for him during the death of his oldest son, way back during their trek together across the plains. Bishop Hughes had just been Nathan back then, and he'd stayed behind the main group to help bury the boy.

And he'd been there again years later when Mary's first daughter had almost died of a fever, giving her a blessing that saved her life. And there were all the little things he did, the wink he gave John when he arrived in the chapel, the clap on the back when they'd built a fence together for a member of the ward, the notebook he'd given John one Christmas, telling him to "write down your deepest thoughts and feelings." John always wondered if he'd share the diary with the bishop one day.

"You turned bitter water into pure water," John said, still on his knees, his face turned upward. "You can turn me into something better, too."

There were times, horrible moments, when John *liked* being a man. He would think of Bishop Hughes and imagine all sorts of abominable things that required two masculine bodies. But he remembered clearly the verse which proclaimed, "If a man also lie with mankind, as he lieth with a woman…" He *couldn't* be with the bishop if he stayed a man. So John was willing to make the ultimate sacrifice and become a woman.

The idea brought the trace of a smile to his lips. He who would give his life for a friend showed the greatest love of all. Becoming a woman was almost the same thing. It absolutely proved John's love.

And if John could love this deeply, then why couldn't God perform another miracle here in the desert? He'd brought the seagulls, hadn't he?

There was a timid knock at the door. John stood up and let Elaine in. "Are you all right?"

"I'm just praying to make a decision that is best for all of us."

"Do you think…" She stopped. "Do you think maybe what's best is that we don't take a fourth wife?"

John's mouth fell open. To flout God's will, to flout Bishop Hughes's will… John would do anything the bishop asked, no matter how painful. He had asked once in private to wash the bishop's feet, and the bishop had allowed it. John still dreamed about that day.

"I'm sorry, husband," Elaine said, seeing his dismay. She left the room, quietly closing the door behind her.

But the idea of rebellion left an odd taste in John's mouth, and not an altogether unpleasant one. What *if*? Maybe he should walk back to the church. Perhaps Bishop Hughes was still there.

John wiped his face and straightened his clothes. He opened the bedroom door and walked back to the kitchen. "I need to talk to the bishop," he said. The women looked at each other carefully. Little Susan tugged at Mary's skirt. Albert tried to sneak a cookie while the mothers weren't paying attention.

John walked back to the church and knocked on Bishop Hughes's door. He felt a wave of relief when the door opened and he saw the bishop standing there.

"My, my," said Bishop Hughes. "Have you made a decision already?"

"Bishop Hughes, I've come to make a confession. Maybe my faith isn't the size of a mustard seed. Perhaps I am not righteous enough to deserve a fourth wife."

The bishop's brow furrowed, and he ushered John into the office. "Is there sin in your life you need to talk about?" he asked. "Something…sexual you do with your wives?" He leaned forward over his desk toward John.

John had meant to be calm and collected, but now he found himself crying, and he was deeply ashamed. He felt as he had that day with the streetwalker. "What is it, my friend?" Bishop Hughes asked, moving over and putting his hand on John's shoulder. "Nothing could be so terrible."

John shook his head. "I am married to the wrong woman, the wrong women," he said. "The wrong person."

The bishop looked confused. "Helen and Isabel are only suggestions. You can marry whoever you like."

"No," John said, shaking his head again. "The person I want is already married."

Bishop Hughes removed his hand. "Oh?" He looked out the window blankly.

John cried more heavily, but this time the bishop walked back over to his chair and sat down.

"Do you want to tell me who she is?" Bishop Hughes asked, a little coldly.

"You're breaking my heart," John sobbed. "Please don't hate me. It's…it's you I want to marry." He put his face in his hands. He couldn't bear to see Bishop Hughes's expression. Why had he said such a thing? Perhaps he would be forced to give up all his wives now. He'd be left with nothing.

What if the bishop told someone else? John was willing to suffer the humiliation of becoming a woman, but could he endure having everyone *know* what he wanted? A private grief, no matter how deep, had to be better than a public one.

He wished he were dead.

John felt a hand on his shoulder again and looked up. Bishop Hughes was standing over him, but then he kneeled, putting his hand instead on John's knee. John looked intently into the bishop's face. He didn't look horrified. John's heart began to beat faster.

"John…"

"Bishop…"

"You must know *why* I keep commanding you to get married?"

John frowned.

"I suppose it's quite sinful of me. But I keep imagining you in bed with these women, and it comforts me."

John's heart began to hurt, it was beating so hard. "What do you mean?"

"I have wanted to be with you as well. But since I cannot marry you myself, I order you to marry others."

John swallowed. "But Bishop…you hold the priesthood. You are a righteous man. Perhaps…perhaps you can anoint me with oil and give me a blessing. You can *command* me to become a woman. Then…then you can marry me." He looked hopefully into the bishop's eyes.

Bishop Hughes removed his hand, and John knew he'd gone too far. The bishop would be repulsed by what he'd said.

"I'm not sure I would *like* you if you were a woman," Bishop Hughes said slowly. "But I suppose it's our only chance." He looked at the floor distractedly for a moment, and then he turned to John again. "Yes," he said, nodding. "Yes, we'll do it."

"You'll see that my wives find another husband?"

"Even if I have to marry them myself."

John smiled. It was all going to work out. He'd been faithful, the bishop had been faithful, and God had been full of love and compassion. John had proven himself, and God would be merciful. "Do you have some oil?" he whispered.

Bishop Hughes smiled and produced a tiny vial. He stood behind John's chair, and John felt a wet fingertip touch him on the crown of his head. A shiver went through his body. All he needed was to have faith as a grain of mustard seed. He'd been imprisoned on his mission to Kentucky, for the Church. He had faith.

"In the name of Jesus Christ, and by the power of the Holy Melchizedek priesthood, which I hold, I command you to become a woman, for your male body to become a female body, according to the love and faith we both have."

Bishop Hughes concluded in the name of the Father, and of the Son, and of the Holy Ghost.

John felt a tingle in his chest, a trembling in his groin. When Bishop Hughes removed his hands from the top of his head, John turned to look up at him, smiling. "Thank you! Oh, thank you! Now—"

He stopped when he saw the look on the bishop's face, and his heart skipped a beat. All he'd needed was faith as a grain of mustard seed, he thought desperately. Surely, he had that much faith. Yes, yes, he was certain he did. He quickly fingered his chest and grabbed his crotch.

But Bishop Hughes was staring at him in horror, and, realizing now what the future held in store for him for the rest of his life, John started crying in despair.

The bishop turned and walked away.

Kolob Abbey

Back in my mortal days, I was a regular PBS viewer. I especially loved BBC productions. You could always catch me watching *Sherlock Holmes* or *Inspector Morse* or *Prime Suspect*. I even liked their comedies, such as *The Vicar of Dibley* and *Are You Being Served?*

But I have to say my favorite programs were *Upstairs, Downstairs* and *Downton Abbey*. Monthly donations to PBS were deducted from my debit card. I was a reasonably intelligent man and liked to promote good television that would raise the overall level of thought in the world.

But I wasn't a snob or anything. I went to the gym daily and worked out to keep my body in shape. I taught Sunday School at the Episcopal church I attended after being excommunicated by the Mormons. I volunteered twice a month at the homeless shelter soup kitchen in Minneapolis. I mowed the lawns of two elderly neighbors in the summer and shoveled their walks in the winter.

I didn't make a lot as a social worker, but I gave $300 every month to a different charity. I had served a two-year mission in Nigeria for the LDS Church when I was nineteen, and after graduating BYU a few years later, spent another year in Africa in the Peace Corps.

I'll admit that part of my motive then was to avoid the issue of marriage, and when I returned to Minnesota, I made an appointment with my bishop and told him he was going to have to remove my name from the records because I was going to a gay bar that coming weekend and never looking back.

He chose to have the stake president hold a court instead. I still believed in God, still believed in Jesus, still wanted to be a good person. I studied several other faiths and eventually ended up an Episcopalian.

The brass bell above my desk rang now, as it usually did about this time of morning, and I put away my journal and headed out of my bedroom.

Walking down the marble hallway to the master bedroom, I continued reflecting on how I'd ended up here. Over the years, I'd helped build four houses for Habitat for Humanity. I picked up trash in parks. I pulled up invasive species of weeds as well. I fell in love with Max, and we spent thirty-one years together, until that fateful night when I tried to drive home from a political rally in the fog.

I rammed into the back of that truck so quickly and forcefully that to be honest, I wasn't even aware what happened. I saw a tunnel with a light at the end, and I felt confused because I seemed to be walking now instead of driving. When had I left the car? I was afraid I'd fallen asleep at the wheel and so tried to wake myself but couldn't.

Once in the light, my grandparents greeted me warmly, my mother was there, some aunts and uncles and cousins, and several of my friends who'd died over the years. I realized at that point what had happened, and I didn't particularly mind being dead. I felt a brief stab of regret over leaving Max, but I knew somehow in my heart that he'd be okay. I was in heaven, and I felt such love that I understood what the saying "being on cloud nine" meant for the first time. I felt I could float on this wave of love forever.

That's when the escorts came. After the short reunion with my loved ones, I was taken to Spirit Prison, where I was given lessons until Judgment Day and the First Resurrection. You see, it turned out the Mormon Church was true.

The members still had some of the doctrine wrong, of course, since humans were so fallible. It was okay for women to wear pants. Coffee wasn't a sin. And gays weren't really abominations. They didn't get sent to Outer Darkness or even the Telestial Kingdom, unless they warranted such things for other reasons.

I ended up with a verdict better than I might have expected. I wasn't sent to the Terrestrial Kingdom with the "good people of the Earth." It was determined I'd exhibited exemplary virtue and compassion, despite my many faults, and I somehow made it into the Celestial Kingdom. Here, though, is where the traditional LDS doctrine did come into play.

Because I hadn't married in the temple, I wasn't worthy of godhood itself. I was only capable of becoming a "ministering angel." I was assured, of course, that this was no trivial accomplishment. Only the most select second-class citizens ever gained such stature. Yes, there was class distinction in heaven. There was nothing wrong with recognizing that some people were inherently better than others. Second class was certainly better than third class, or fourth class, or eightieth class, or three hundred and fifty-seventh class.

There were a lot of classes in heaven.

"James, could you come to my room?" That was Caleb, the god I was assigned to, calling me on my Communicator, which was hanging from my belt. I'd always been Jimmy on Earth, but here in the Celestial Kingdom, things were a bit formal.

Caleb wasn't usually impatient, but I must have been dawdling in my reflective state of mind. Caleb himself had seemed preoccupied the last few days, and I suppose that had put me in a similar mood.

I passed Calpurnia in the hallway and nodded politely to her. Cal and Cal they'd been on Earth, but they too went by their full names here in the Celestial Kingdom. They'd both been black in mortality and were a little surprised to find themselves still black in the hereafter.

They'd been proud African Americans, but as devout Mormons, they couldn't help but believe their skin would become white and delightsome at some point. It took them a few years to fully get over it.

I wasn't assigned to Caleb until well after that, but he'd confided it to me a few days ago. On *their* planet, they insisted on creating seven different skin colors so it would be harder for any one to claim superiority. Even as a disinterested onlooker, however, I could see clearly that the green humans were well on their way to dominance down below.

But Caleb was in charge. That was a deistic problem. I was just a valet.

The house was huge, taking up forty acres. There were several wings simply for the wives. Calpurnia was number one, but after Judgment Day, there'd been many more weddings, to women who'd been worthy in Earth life but who either hadn't had the chance to marry in the temple or whose husbands hadn't made it to the top with them.

There were apparently a lot more righteous women than men back on Earth. It always seemed to be related to testosterone, and holding us accountable for a hormone we didn't choose seemed unfair.

But then I wasn't the Supreme Judge.

I knocked gently on Caleb's door, and he called out for me to enter. "Good morning, Caleb," I said, smiling brightly. "How are you?"

"I'm fine, thank you, James," he said from his bed. "Six more births last night. Always got to be making more spirit babies, even though we made billions before that planet ever cooled."

"It's good you have perfect stamina," I replied. I pulled the sheet down to let Caleb sit up and swing his legs over the side of the bed. It had four towering bedposts, intricately carved. A massive headboard joined the two posts at the head of the bed. Tyler, who I'd known since Spirit Prison, had crafted it, as he'd made the bed frames for over half the wives.

Carving was a solitary job, and occasionally when we had lunch together when our days off coincided, Tyler would express a wish that he had more direct interaction with the gods. I'd always smile politely. This morning, our god Caleb was wearing a white nightgown. It made his dark skin almost shine in contrast.

Caleb stood and held out his arms, and I untied the nightgown and pulled it off him. He was a fine specimen of a man, though never having worked directly with any other gods, I couldn't really make a fair comparison. Probably most gods were in pretty good shape.

As usual, I let my eyes linger a bit too long on his genitals. I was still gay, after all, and there was nothing quite like looking at a perfect penis every day on the job.

It was a penis in the Celestial Kingdom, not a dick.

I had to admit, things could be worse.

"Okay, okay, James, enough of that. You'll make me get an erection, and you know I don't like to get hard till after lunch when I start visiting the West Wing."

"Sorry, Caleb." I slipped a toga over his head and pulled it tight around his waist with a maroon rope. Caleb wore all sorts of clothes, pants and shirt sometimes, a suit, a blouse and kilt, a dress, and several different types of robes, all depending on his mood.

Part of my job was to anticipate his mood and choose the right wardrobe for the day even before he suggested anything. When you've been working for someone over three billion years, you learn to pick up on those things.

As I finished, Caleb put one hand on my shoulder and sighed.

"What is it, sir?"

"I was just thinking this arrangement somehow doesn't seem fair."

I raised an eyebrow. "I very much enjoy working for you, Caleb."

Caleb chuckled and shook his head. "What I mean is that you get to see my penis every day, and after all these years, I've never had an opportunity to see yours."

"Sir?"

Caleb sat down on his bed and patted the sheet next to him for me to sit as well. I sat down reluctantly.

"It's something I've never confided in you yet, though we've known each other all these years. It obviously came out in the trial on Judgment Day, but you didn't know me then and so probably didn't pay very much attention."

I looked at him questioningly.

He sighed again. "They told us in church that being gay was a mortal experience, that it wasn't an eternal identity. I think about that promise every day. Not once in Earth life did I have sex with a man. Not once. And it paid off." He waved his arms around the room. "But still. It's hard to go *forever* without having what you want."

"Sir, they'll be waiting for you at breakfast." I started to get up, but Caleb put his hand on my knee.

"Yes, and they'll have my favorite foods, as usual. I know." He shook his head and started picking at the frayed end of the rope around his waist. "I always loved bacon and still do. I always loved fried eggs and still do. I always loved hash browns and still do."

"Caleb…"

"And I've always loved men." He took my hand and squeezed it. "It's not a matter of temptation. There's no temptation anymore. But I still like what I like. And after having you dress me for 3,614,379,401 years, I've just *got* to see your penis at least once." He motioned with his hand. "May I?"

"Caleb, you know I'll always do whatever you command me to do."

"Do I have to command it?" he asked sadly.

I thought back to that day so many years ago when Caleb first took me into the house, after we'd spent countless years gathering space dust and forming stars and planets. Once all that preliminary work was done, there weren't many important tasks left for us angels to do.

The gods still had to keep us employed, however, so most of us were transferred to teaching and tending the spirit children. Others made clothes. Some tended the gardens. But Caleb had taken me in to work for him personally. I figured it was because he knew I never much liked children, and he was being kind. Even now, I realized he surely didn't want to see *my* penis, just *any* penis. It wasn't very flattering. I felt as if I were scratching an itch for him.

Which I sometimes did when he was coming out of the shower.

I stood up, and Caleb smiled. I was wearing a basic blue robe today, and I lifted it up over my waist. Caleb's eyes went straight to my pubic area.

"Could you…?" he asked.

"It's been a long time," I said. "You know we can't even masturbate up here. So my plumbing hasn't had to work in quite a while." I closed my eyes and concentrated, allowing myself to fantasize for the first time in eons. I'd almost forgotten how, but I suppose it was like riding a bike. I thought about Max, and two minutes later, I was hard.

"It's beautiful," Caleb breathed. He moved closer and stared.

I felt like Sally Hemings.

Just when Caleb was about to touch it, I cleared my throat. "You know, sir, that you still have to answer to *your* god."

Caleb pulled away and stared glumly at the floor. "It doesn't quite seem fair, does it? I worked so hard during Earth life, and I've done nothing but prove myself over and over these past few billion years. I've been *perfect* all this time. I'm a *god*. Why can't *I* make the rules?"

I shrugged. "Heavenly Father always insisted that the laws weren't his, that there are natural eternal laws we must all abide." I lowered my robe, my penis making it poke out like a tent. I felt slightly embarrassed.

"Do you think he was telling the truth?"

"I can't say," I said slowly. "He's never let us meet *his* god. We just have to take his word for it."

"It doesn't seem fair," Caleb repeated.

I began to feel a little irritated and said, "Well, what about me, sir? My entire eternity is based on what I did during a few measly years on Earth. It's like taking a random two minutes out of a single day in the life of a kindergartner and basing where he goes to graduate school on those two minutes." Even though Earth life was so long ago, since so much depended on it, we still found ourselves making analogies based on our experiences from that brief period.

Caleb nodded. "I suppose I accept the status quo without questioning," he said. "That's part of what got me here in the first place."

"And I rebelled against the status quo," I pointed out, "and ended up an eternal servant."

"Well, when you think about it," Caleb said, a little defensively, "*I'm* serving billions and billions of spirits by giving them spirit bodies and sending them down to Anregan, and then by listening to their neverending prayers." He held his head. "It's like a continual ringing in my ears every second of the day."

"Uh-huh." I knew he recorded over 90% of those prayers with a device one of his other servants created and handed them off to yet more staff in the outlying buildings on the estate. He'd named the estate Kolob, after his god's home world. He'd named his own planet Anregan, after a science fiction novel he'd read as a teenager.

Caleb spent maybe two or three hours every morning directly responding to the people on his planet clamoring for his help. He may have been gay, but he seemed much more intent on his afternoon duties "serving" his wives, seven a day.

I looked at Caleb sharply. I wondered if he'd been led to believe that if he had enough sex with enough goddesses, eventually his homosexuality would go away up here, just as on Earth we'd been told that serving as a missionary or marrying a woman would make the gay go away back there.

I shuddered. Was an eternity having sex with spouses you weren't attracted to what heaven was all about? It sounded more like hell to me. Even celibacy was better than that.

I wished they'd let me see Max, but he hadn't been quite as generous with his charity work on Earth and had only merited the Terrestrial Kingdom. We did get to Skype, but some days that just wasn't enough. I wanted to hold him now.

We were told that technically, even the lower degrees of heaven, the Terrestrial and Telestial Kingdoms, were hell because while there, one was separated eternally from Heavenly Father. Only in the Celestial Kingdom could one see and interact with the god who'd sent us to Earth. That was supposed to mean something, being in the *real* heaven.

But Caleb and Calpurnia and the other wives were the only ones who had contact with him. For the rest of us, Caleb had become our new boss. It was he to whom we reported.

As nice as he usually was, the place still sometimes felt a little like hell. I'd resigned myself to that brass bell in my tiny bedroom, but now I wondered if that was the right decision.

"Thanks for letting me see your penis, James," Caleb said, standing up.

"Thanks for letting me see *yours*," I replied. "It's almost as nice as Max's."

Caleb froze and stared at me. "You—you mean there are *better* penises than mine?"

"I've seen dozens of them."

Caleb continued staring.

"Not that yours isn't quite impressive. I'm just saying."

"I'm going to breakfast. Be back here in an hour to help me change into my work clothes."

"Yes, sir."

Caleb dismissed me with a wave of his hand, and I headed back down the hallway and downstairs to my room. I picked up a book about life in the six hundredth year of the Millennium and started reading. We could only read "good" books with "appropriate" content. There certainly hadn't been enough of those written back on Earth. I went through all of those in a couple of decades.

Fortunately, many of the people sent to the Terrestrial Kingdom were able to develop their writing skills, and they produced more books for us to read. Some of them helped provide the infrastructure we relied on up here in the

Celestial Kingdom, even if they weren't technically "ministering angels" themselves. For instance, they helped provide and sustain the communication devices we used daily. They helped produce the cloth that we then sewed into clothing up here.

If it took a village to raise a child, it took a whole nation to sustain a god. Those of us in the Celestial Kingdom were awarded the most select of the servant positions, but even with twenty thousand servants, we weren't enough to serve one god, plus just over twenty-five hundred goddesses, and countless spirit children. We simply had to outsource some of the more mundane work.

Max had once slipped me a handwritten note inside the packaging for some materials to be turned into a new pair of sandals for Caleb. Though we saw each other on the Ethernet once a week, I still felt a tremendous thrill go through my body when I saw the note. It said simply, "Yours always, Max."

I wondered if I should abdicate my position here and ask to be sent down to a lower kingdom. I'd asked that very question almost as soon as I'd arrived eons ago and was given a blunt no in response. But now I questioned whether I needed to accept that answer. Even now, after all these years making friends with other angels, my weekly chats with Max were the only thing that gave me the strength to go on.

I wrote a little more in my journal and was back in Caleb's bedroom in time to see him come back from breakfast. He did not look as if he'd had a good meal.

"Are you feeling well, sir?" I asked. It was a stupid question. Gods never became ill. Hash browns were never burned. I knew perfectly well what the problem was.

Caleb glared at me. I remembered reading stories from the Old Testament where God had acted petulantly or angrily, and it always bothered me that a perfect being could behave in ways that seemed so imperfect. Even Caleb had his moods. Earth life was the single most decisive and formative influence on our character, stronger than the influence of the Pre-Existence before we gained physical bodies, and stronger than anything that happened after Judgment Day.

That's precisely why what we did on Earth mattered so much. In the Pre-Existence, we were like sand on a beach. During Earth life, we were molten glass easily molded into almost any form. In the afterlife, we were pretty much the vessel or object we'd been shaped into while in the furnace of Earthly experience, just polished a little.

I accepted that this meant I would always be gay. If I had to be celibate, being gay or straight didn't make much difference. But for a god like Caleb…

"Sir, what are you going to do?" I asked softly.

"What do you mean?" He held out his arms again, and I took off the toga and started putting on his blue pinstriped suit. Caleb lifted his legs at the appropriate times as I slid the pants on him and bent his arms so I could get him into his starched white shirt.

"It's one thing to suppress who you really are for six or seven billion years. But you realize, you have *hundreds* of billions of years still ahead of you. *Trillions* of billions. You're still a relatively new god."

Caleb's gaze hardened. "I'm a god, and I'm going to do what gods do."

I put a knot in his tie.

"No more penis envy?" I said with a smile.

He shot me a dirty look. "Do you want to work in the nursery for a million years?"

"No, sir."

Caleb looked at himself in the mirror and nodded authoritatively at what he saw. Then he started toward the door. "Folks are going to get some tough love answers to their prayers today." Just before he reached the hallway, he turned back and said, "Be here at 11:45 to dress me for lunch." Then he went on without even a wave of his hand.

I had some free time now, one of the perks of this special position. I went back to my room and sat at my desk, looking up at the brass bell for the longest time. I thought about my mortal expectations of immortality. I figured gods and probably angels could just blink like Barbara Eden and create things out of nothing, but even gods didn't have that kind of power.

We could teleport in a beam of light like they did on *Star Trek*, something apparent from the days Joseph Smith described his angelic visitations. But most of what we did here was drudge work just like back on Earth. The priesthood wasn't nearly as big a deal as it had been made out to be.

I remembered a time when Max and I were trying to refinance our home and had to get a new appraisal. We owned a hundred-year-old house in downtown Minneapolis and had been doing some renovations, taking out the old furnace but not having yet replaced it with a new one. There were also some holes in the kitchen wall from some other work we'd done.

The bank had balked at the results, saying they couldn't possibly refinance a home in that condition. I had prayed for help and had experienced some fleeting self-doubt over the kind of help Heavenly Father would give an apostate Mormon.

Still, Max and I had gone to another institution and tried again. Only this time we put up a shelf in the kitchen and covered the holes with a row of large cereal boxes. And we bought a few grills and affixed them to various walls in the house and pretended they were part of our heating system.

We got the loan.

And despite the blatant dishonesty, I made it to the Celestial Kingdom.

It was two more days before my day off, when I would be allowed to talk to Max. I took a deep breath and walked to the servants' library, logging onto a computer as nonchalantly as I could. Some of the others in the room may have noticed, but no one said anything. Max was already on the ether, not having as many restrictions on his time, and I made my request quickly. "What are your GPS coordinates?" He seemed puzzled but gave me the information. I blew him a kiss and logged out.

The next part would be trickier. I returned to Caleb's room and gathered a hunter green cloak and his favorite red hat. Then I made my way into the East Wing to the far end where the transporter room lay. The angel manning the post, Michael, put down his magazine and sat up straight when I entered, relaxing a little when he saw I was alone.

"Caleb has to make a short trip," I explained. "He asked me to meet him here with his accessories."

Michael nodded.

"There's a little clutter out in the hall," I said uncomfortably. "Do you think…?"

"I'll get right on it," Michael said, jumping up from his seat.

The moment he was out of sight, I ran over to the control panel and input the coordinates to Max's home on the planet where he was stationed light years away. I knew I only had seconds. I pushed the button, giving myself a two-second time delay, and ran to the platform. As the light filled my eyes, I could see Michael returning with a look of horror on his face.

But I'd left him the cloak and the hat, so at least he'd have something to offer Caleb.

The Waters of Redemption

I remember growing up and hearing of terrible earthquakes in faraway lands, of catastrophic hurricanes and forest fires. I remembered how just a few years ago, in 1972, there was a string of tornadoes in Ohio that destroyed hundreds of homes. But Mom always said, "The Lord will protect his saints."

"Then why do Mormons need a year's supply of food and provisions?" I asked.

"That's for when there's a worldwide disaster at the end of times. But until then, the Lord will spare us."

The idea made me uncomfortable. "God loves us more than other people?"

Mom laughed and shook her head. "It isn't a matter of love. It's a covenant. We obey his word, and he protects us."

I thought about the Jews, and how they must have felt betrayed by the Holocaust. Did we only *think* we were on God's side? Even if other people, say in Bangladesh, weren't Mormons, was that really their fault? Just how many missionaries were there in Bangladesh, after all? It didn't seem fair for God to wipe out 300,000 people in a cyclone there just because the people were ignorant through no fault of their own.

Still, if it were true, it was nice to know I was on the Lord's team. Having grown up in Rexburg, I'd always felt privileged to live in the same town as Ricks College. It wasn't as prestigious as BYU, but it was still a Church school, and I felt special to have been raised in its shadow, the way I felt special to be born into a Mormon family.

I belonged to an elite. Mormons were a mere fraction of the world's population, yet we were the only ones with the truth. The weight of responsibility was awesome, but the relief was great, too.

I was thinking of these things as my two younger sisters watched Saturday morning TV, enjoying cartoons even as teenagers, but now I went outside and sat on the lawn. It was a hot summer day, early in June. The nation's bicentennial would take place in just one more month.

It was wonderful to live in the Promised Land, too, another accident of birth, but I knew it wasn't entirely an accident. God had put me in a Mormon family, in America, because I was a special spirit in the Pre-Existence.

The only trouble was that along with my special status came a special trial. God had made me gay, to try my faith. I'd just graduated from high school a couple of weeks ago, and in the fall I'd start my first year at Ricks before going on a mission. I was still a virgin, of course, though I was plagued with the sin of masturbation.

And I thought about guys a lot, like my gym coach who'd taken a shower with the P.E. class once after a hard workout, and like Clint Eastwood in *The Good, the Bad, and the Ugly.* He was so dirty in that movie I wanted to see him take a shower, too.

I spent a lot of time in the shower myself, staying after the rest of the team was clean and dressed. I always kept imagining more dirt under my fingernails, more sweat under my armpits. I scrubbed my face till it was raw, but I just wanted to be clean. I took a shower every Saturday night and then again on Sunday morning, needing two to be ready for church.

Obviously, I was a little concerned about my upcoming mission. Would being with guys non-stop for two years help me or hurt me? Maybe after a year of classes at Ricks, it wouldn't even be an issue anymore. I'd be going to Institute, too, after all, receiving adult-level LDS instruction.

I wondered how other gay people handled the problem. Certainly, many of them failed at the challenge. But that was because they weren't part of this special group of people. You never heard about gay Mormons because clearly those afflicted with this weakness found strength in the gospel and overcame it. There was no "I" in "team," and there was no "I" in "Mormon," either. You worked for the good of the whole Church, and it in turn worked for your good, too.

"Hey, Danny what'cha doing?" It was Carson, the boy next door, who I also wouldn't have minded seeing dripping wet sometime, though, to be honest, a lot of boys fell into that category.

"Just enjoying the sun," I said.

"Want some company?"

"Sure." I patted the grass beside me. I loved lying on my back in the sun. I could feel the energy beneath me, ants and beetles and worms, but also the life-force of the grass itself, and of the Earth. I felt a part of the universe at times like this.

"How come you're not working?" Carson asked, plopping down beside me on the lawn.

"How come *you're* not?" I countered.

He laughed. "I figure I'll be part of the working world the rest of my life. This is my one last summer to be a kid."

I nodded, though I felt his response was a little juvenile. I had no particular desire to man a Laundromat or wash dishes myself, but I could at least have started summer classes at Ricks. It was only that part of me felt unclean, and I didn't want to contaminate that great campus.

I thought maybe doing baptisms for the dead in the temple in Boise would help, so I'd scheduled time next Saturday and planned to keep doing it until my soul felt as white as my temple clothes.

But really, I felt too unclean even to clean myself. The baptisms wouldn't be washing away *my* sins, after all, but those of people long dead. Partaking of the sacrament every Sunday was supposed to be the upkeep mode of baptismal renewal, but half a bite of bread and a thimbleful of water didn't do much for me emotionally. It was good to take part in a group ritual, but I doubted anyone else had to repent of the degree of sin I did.

"What are you studying in the fall?" I asked.

"Nothing special. Just my freshman courses. English, math, that kind of thing."

"You're going to wait to declare a major till after your mission?"

"I…I don't know if I want to go on a mission," Carson said slowly.

It was unfathomable. "Don't you believe in the Church?"

Carson leaned on one elbow and looked directly at me. "Aren't there times you just want to do your own thing, live your own life?"

"Well, yes, but—"

He put his hand on my arm. "Don't you sometimes want something the Church says you can't have?"

Oh my god. What was he getting at? We had beat off together once on a camping trip, but we hadn't touched each other. It had been a guy thing, not a gay thing, and that had been years ago. Was he saying now that he really liked me?

"What…what do *you* want?" I asked, trembling just a little. I'd never been in love with Carson, but to be able to talk to another person about what I was feeling would be such a relief. Not to be alone anymore would be a revelation.

Carson looked me in the eyes for a long moment, his hand still resting on my arm. I felt myself starting to get an erection.

Carson looked away. "I can't say it. I simply can't say it."

"It's okay," I said gently, putting my hand on top of his. "I'm gay, too."

"What?" Carson sat upright, withdrawing his hand quickly.

"Isn't that what you were about to tell me?"

"I was *going* to say I want to boink your sister but that I don't want to marry her."

"Oh."

There was a realization in Carson's eyes. "Oh, Jeez. Do you have a *crush* on me? That is so gross, man." He looked like he'd just smelled rotting garbage. "What's it like to be a son of perdition?"

"Carson, how can you say that? You know me."

"Apparently not."

"I haven't done anything, you know. I'm still clean."

Carson shook his head. I knew I was lying, and Carson did, too. "Danny, you can't be gay and be clean. It's a contradiction of terms. You're the reason Sodom and Gomorrah were destroyed. You're the reason places like San Francisco are going to be destroyed." He thought for a moment, and I struggled for something to say.

"Carson, can't you…help me?"

"Help you? How? If you were good, you wouldn't be gay."

"But I want to go on a mission, get married in the temple, raise a righteous family."

"Then you have to stop being a pervert."

"That's exactly what I want," I protested.

"Obviously not as much as you want sin, or you'd be straight."

"Do you think I should ask to be excommunicated so I can be baptized again? Do you think that would help?"

"Baptism only washes away sins if you repent."

"But Carson, I never chose this. It—it just happened. I haven't acted on it. Ever."

"Then how do you know you're gay?"

I shrugged. "Well…I have thoughts…"

"Oh, Jeez. Have you been fantasizing about *me*?"

Actually, I hadn't. Maybe once or twice, but he wasn't really my type. And yet, I suspected telling him that would only alienate him more. So I said nothing.

"Jeez."

It was disappointing not to get support, but perhaps I could still get some good advice. Whether or not he planned to go on a mission, he was nevertheless an active priest in our ward. "Do you think I should move to San Francisco for a year or two and get it out of my system?"

Carson shook his head. "It's like being an alcoholic," he said. "The more you drink, the worse your disease becomes.

You're an alcoholic who's never had a beer. So the only way you can avoid ending up in the gutter is by never taking that first drink."

I'd heard about AA meetings. I wondered if there was a Gays Anonymous group, too. Was my life going to be an endless series of frustrated temptations? My choices were to be miserable *in* the gutter or forever miserable on the *edge* of the gutter?

Well, if those were the choices, I'd choose to be on the edge of disaster rather than in the midst of it. I wanted to be with my people, and if going to clandestine meetings was the only way to achieve it, then I'd do it. I'd have to talk to the bishop tomorrow after church and see what he suggested.

As awful as it was to have my secret out now with Carson, it also somehow felt liberating. I could finally talk to the bishop. He wouldn't disfellowship me. He'd help me to become stronger. The Church must have *some* program for the few people like me who existed. The Church wouldn't just abandon us to the devil without a fight.

"Thanks, Carson. You're a pal."

"Jeez."

He got up and walked back to his house, shaking his head. I wondered if he'd ever come back. There were bound to be a few insensitive saints out there, but to be saints meant supporting each other as we all faced our trials. The rest of the Church wouldn't be like that. Carson's reaction was what I'd feared, but now that I'd endured it, I realized it was only an isolated incident and that I could take it.

I couldn't wait to talk to the bishop tomorrow.

It was still an hour till lunch, and I was antsy, so I stood up and started walking through the neighborhood. This section on the northern end of town was old, with small houses despite the large families. But it was clean. People here washed their cars, kept their lawns picked up. I could feel the Mormonism emanating from these homes. Our goal as missionaries was to convert enough people so that the saints everywhere could enjoy living in LDS communities like this one.

What must it be like to live in towns where all you had in common with your next-door neighbor was geography? In places like Rexburg, everyone was bound together by a common goal, to reach the Celestial Kingdom and become gods. There were still a few creeps who always caused trouble, but for the most part, people got along. We were all in the same boat, and we were rowing together in unison as a team. That meant we were moving toward our destination faster than other people.

I *had* to overcome this gay thing. I felt like the guy who'd killed the albatross and had to wear the dead bird to save the ship. Only the ship wasn't saved, was it? Everyone else ended up dying because of that one sinner. Maybe they should have thrown him overboard to save the rest of the crew.

"Hey, Cheyenne," I said, seeing one of my schoolmates going out to pick up her mail. Cheyenne had been a junior last year but now would be one of the reigning class this fall.

"Hi, Danny. What's up?"

Cheyenne dropped a letter, and I reached down to pick it up. As I handed it to her, my fingers touched hers. She smiled.

I knew Cheyenne had her eye on me. Other kids had told me, but I could see it for myself, even as oblivious as I normally was toward girls. Suddenly, I got an idea.

"Wanna make out?" I asked bluntly.

"What?"

"The Rivertons are out of town. And I know where they keep their spare key."

"You're horrible," she said, but she was smiling. "Let me bring this inside first."

A few minutes later, we were walking up to the Rivertons' house a street over. I lifted a small pot with a red geranium and picked up the front door key. And then we were inside. We looked around the living room, but not too nosily. I motioned for Cheyenne to sit down, and I sat right beside her, my leg pressing against hers. "I'm a good girl," she said.

"I know. That's why I like you." I felt like a heel, but I knew she wanted to kiss me, so this would be good for her as well as for me. I leaned over and saw her brace herself, but as soon as my lips touched hers, she moved forward to meet me head on.

I'd never kissed before and wasn't quite sure I was doing it right. It was oddly satisfying and yet just a little disgusting. I wondered if Cheyenne had brushed her teeth after breakfast.

I felt her hands on my back and decided I needed to put mine on hers as well.

We kissed for several minutes, and I was relieved to discover I felt the slightest stirring in my groin.

Cheyenne broke off the kiss. "We…we could go lie down," she said softly. Then she blushed. "Not have sex or anything," she added quickly. "Just to be more comfortable."

Right then, I knew I could seduce her, and my erection grew stronger. I could be cured today. Saved. My heart started beating faster.

"Cheyenne," I said slowly. "There's something I have to tell you."

Her eyes narrowed. "Yes?"

"I'm gay." I felt my face burning. "I'm a virgin, of course. But…but I think…being with you might…"

She looked at me for a long moment. Then she stood up. I felt like a complete rat.

She offered her hand. "Come on," she said.

I took her hand, and we walked deeper into the house until we came to the Rivertons' bedroom. I wasn't sure I wanted to do this. We stood beside the bed, and Cheyenne began unbuttoning her blouse. I pulled off my T-shirt and then waited for her to catch up. When she began pulling off her shorts, I unbuckled my belt.

We stood there looking at each other in the dim light filtering through the closed curtains. She smiled as she looked at my erection, and I smiled, too. I couldn't be too far gone yet. Maybe I was being caught in time, learning to drink coffee instead of alcohol. Still sinning, but less seriously.

Cheyenne lay on top of the covers, and I climbed over next to her. I let my hand touch her stomach and then move slowly up to her breasts. When she touched my left nipple, I jumped and we both giggled. Then she reached lower and put her fingers around my penis.

We continued caressing each other for maybe five or six more minutes, but it wasn't long before I knew I had to get inside of her. I climbed on top, and we kissed again.

But as soon as my eyes closed, I saw Samuel. He was a boy who lived on this same street, a boy I really did have a crush on. He wasn't on the team but could have been if he'd wanted. He had great pecs, and dark stubble on his face by mid-morning. As soon as I saw him in my mind, I felt my penis throb so hard it hurt.

If I thought of him while I was inside Cheyenne, would that help me or hurt me? I was so turned on I had to do *something*, but I knew I needed to look at Cheyenne. Yet now I was afraid to open my eyes. I *liked* seeing Samuel.

Fumbling about with my eyes closed, I tried to maneuver my penis between Cheyenne's legs. She gasped as I pushed inside of her. Then I slowly started pumping, and Cheyenne whispered my name. And all I could think about was the time in the locker room during P.E. when I saw Samuel bending over. He had on a jock strap, even though he wasn't a jock, and I could see his butt crack so clearly. I wanted inside that ass.

I slowed down and almost stopped. What kind of a person would want to be inside the most disgusting part of the human body? It *had* to be of the devil.

I opened my eyes and saw Cheyenne looking at me intently. Though I'd been only moments from orgasm, seeing her beneath me made me go limp almost immediately. I looked away guiltily.

"Did you come?" she whispered.

I decided to tell her yes so I wouldn't hurt her feelings, but when I looked at her again, I started to cry. One of my tears hit her cheek.

"You couldn't do it, could you?" She pushed me off of her, and I lay on the bed, my hands over my face. "I knew I wasn't risking much. I suppose if we haven't had sex, I'm still a virgin."

"I'm sorry," I said. "You're beautiful, but…" I felt Cheyenne's hand on mine and let out a deep breath. She removed my hands from my face and I looked up at her.

Only to close my eyes instinctively when I felt her spit hit my face.

"Wait'll I tell Stacy about you," Cheyenne said. "She has two brothers on the baseball team. The whole school will know about you by nightfall."

School was over, I thought. I'd never be going back. And yet, to know I could never even show up at my ten-year reunion made me want to cry again. I wondered why Cheyenne hadn't said, "The whole ward will know by tonight." Weren't the same people in my school in my ward, too?

But if Cheyenne still considered herself a virgin, then maybe I was, too. I couldn't be kicked out of the Church just for thinking about Samuel's ass, could I?

I decided I'd better get home and tell my parents before they heard the news from anyone else. Maybe they could get me into therapy. It was clear I couldn't overcome this on my own.

"Cheyenne," I said, "thanks. I—"

"Wash your mouth out."

I nodded.

A second later, we heard a siren a couple of streets over, and then a muffled voice over a loudspeaker. There was never any crime in Rexburg, so Cheyenne and I looked at each other in confusion. Had someone seen us come in here?

We quickly got dressed and went outside. I put the key back under the pot. We heard the siren again, just a street away this time, and then the muffled voice spoke once more, a little more loudly but still not clearly enough to make out. Maybe there was an escaped criminal.

Like me. I knew I should be locked up.

But immediately, I began thinking of what I would do trapped in a tiny cell with another man.

I needed something more severe than prison.

We started walking back to our street, and at the corner, a police officer drove slowly past, blaring his siren for a moment, and then coming on his loudspeaker again. "The Teton dam has collapsed. Get to high ground immediately. The Teton dam has collapsed. Get to high ground immediately."

Cheyenne and I looked at each other in surprise. Then she turned and started running in the direction of Ricks College. I took off for home. I got there as my dad was trying to force Mom into the car. My two sisters were already in back. Mom screamed and pointed at me, and Dad shoved me into the vehicle. We took off seconds later.

We ended up at Ricks, too, one of the highest parts of town, along with everyone else. But the water didn't arrive for a long time. We thought at first maybe there'd been a mistake, or perhaps the water would only be a trickle by the time it got downstream this far.

And then we saw it. A thick, churning, muddy mess going through neighborhood after neighborhood. Some houses were knocked off their foundations. Others had cars rammed into walls. The lucky houses only got three or four feet of muddy water.

And I knew in every fiber of my being this was completely my fault. The water was the color of shit. And I had wanted to get inside Samuel's ass. God had destroyed cities before because of homosexuality. And he was doing it again.

The different towns upstream would be destroyed, too, Wilford, Sugar City, Salem, Hibbard. And all because of me.

God must really hate homosexuals if the sin of one person could warrant such destruction.

I stared at the rushing water, feeling like a murderer. The thought made me stiffen. I probably *was* a murderer. Even with police warnings, surely a few people had been caught in the flood and drowned. And wasn't I in essence some terrorist, blowing up the dam? How could I ever live with myself?

I saw Carson forty yards away, and even from that distance, I could tell he was glaring at me. He knew it was my fault, too. There were maybe ten thousand people on this hillside. All homeless because of me.

Excommunication wasn't even an issue anymore. The situation was much more dire than that. And now I knew I could never tell my parents. I had to take care of this on my own.

I moved off from my family several yards, and then I started making my way downhill. There was only one solution. I would immerse myself in the filthy water and drown. It was the only way to save anyone else. I was clearly damned in any event, so all that mattered were the others.

I hadn't even stopped to try to save Samuel, I realized, having run back home instead. I loved him, and I had abandoned him without a thought? That's what gay love was.

I looked up the hill to see my family one last time. I could see Carson heading in their direction. I hurried my steps.

When I reached the edge of the water, I hesitated. It was only a few feet deep. Even though there was a strong current,

I was afraid I wouldn't be able to drown. I'd have to force my way as far into the churning mess as I could.

I took two steps into the water and was almost knocked off my feet.

I could do this.

I waded out several more yards and was hit by a branch and then by a chair floating by. A dead rat bumped into me. I nodded and walked out further. Then, instinctively taking a deep breath, I started to kneel down to make the water deeper.

"Danny!" I heard a voice calling, muffled because of the sound of the flood. "Danny!"

I turned to look, afraid of seeing my father coming for me. But it wasn't my father. It was Samuel.

"Danny! I'm okay! I'm okay! Don't go out there! I made it out okay!" He waded out a couple of yards and motioned for me to come back to shore. When I hesitated, he walked out another six yards and wrapped his arms around me. "I wanted to look for you earlier, but my family made me stay with them. I couldn't find you in all that big crowd up on the hill. Then I saw you walking down, and I knew you were looking for me."

"I—I—"

"I love you, too." He kissed me full on the lips, just as a heavy log rammed into us, knocking us over. I went under, and my shirt snagged on a branch, the tree starting to carry me away. I felt a strong hand on my arm, and Samuel ripped me back to the surface.

"Let's get out of here."

We made it back to land and collapsed on the grass, covered in a thin layer of mud. Samuel looked at me and smiled, but I felt worse than ever. He thought I'd been thinking of him rather than myself. And even knowing he loved me, how could I ever be happy that he was damned, too?

We didn't say anything else for a long while. We lay beside each other, my head on his shoulder, watching the muddy water destroy our town.

When night fell, we made our way back up the hill. The only lights still working were on campus. We'd have to sleep in the gym or some hallway for who knew how long. Samuel and I sat together, watching the thick crowds move slowly around us.

And then a miracle happened. Around 11:00, the first buses from Salt Lake began arriving, with hundreds of volunteers coming to help the town clean up. They looked like angels, and I overheard one of the men saying, "This is what it means to belong."

Samuel took my hand, and I looked at him. He looked out at the throngs about us and shook his head. "We belong to each other," he whispered.

We belonged to Satan, I thought, but part of me decided that perhaps that wasn't so bad, if Samuel would always be there to hold my hand.

"We destroyed the town," I said softly, wondering if love could survive such sin.

Samuel shook his head again. "Our love will save the world."

I sighed wearily. I knew he was mistaken. Wickedness never was happiness. But if wickedness was all we had, I would make it as comforting to Samuel as I could.

"I'm all covered in stinky mud," I said. "So it won't hurt me any to get inside your stinky ass." I forced a smile. "Can I?"

Samuel nodded. "We won't be able to clean up afterward."

He squeezed my hand and we began walking, searching for a dark corner.

Being dirty throughout eternity suddenly started sounding like a good thing.

Still True

I wished I were a movie director. One of my favorite films was *Groundhog Day*. Justin and I used to watch it at least once a year, though never in February. On our second date, after we'd just watched the movie for the first time, he said, "Fletcher, that's the way eternity is going to be for us. We'll get to redo everything as many times as it takes till we get everything right."

"Reincarnation?" I asked.

"No. Just practice. Practice makes perfect, and we're commanded to be perfect."

I must have frowned in response because he then added, "Fletcher, we'll get to make love for the first time a million times. We'll have our first kiss a million more. And you'll hear me say 'I love you' with this same intensity a million more times beyond that."

I laughed. "You love me? Justin, it's only our second date."

He took my hand and looked deep into my eyes. "Are you telling me you don't feel the same way?"

I stared back into his eyes and knew he was right. We both lived in Salt Lake but had never met until a Sunstone symposium a few weeks earlier. But whether it was two soulmates uniting victoriously, or a simple chemical reaction in my brain, I knew I loved him, too. We made love for the second time that night, and it was just as wonderful as the first time.

Despite our instant connection, we managed to wait six months before moving in together. That had been fifteen years ago. And it had been a mostly wonderful fifteen years. We argued perhaps once a year, and each time it was devastating, realizing we wouldn't always live in perfect harmony. But we also resolved our differences quickly, too, and the arguments were more trivial each year. The past three years, we hadn't argued at all.

Well, once. When Justin told me he wanted to stop his chemotherapy and let Nature take its course, I argued. He'd won that one, though to be honest, it probably wouldn't have made much difference in any event. Pancreatic cancer wasn't easy to combat. He died a little over four months ago.

His last words were, "We're legally married. That means one day you can do proxy work in the temple and we'll be married forever."

"Honey, the Church isn't true," I whispered back.

"I want to be with you forever," he insisted. "Promise me you'll go to the temple once the Prophet has a revelation."

"I promise, Justin." Who wouldn't say anything to comfort a dying man?

"I love you, Fletcher."

"I love you, too."

Then he closed his eyes and died. Just like that. It didn't seem real. I felt like a participant on a reality show, when the "reality" was scripted. Now the cameras were off, and it was time for Justin to quit playing his role of sick person. It was time for us to leave the hospital and go home.

I signed some papers donating Justin's body to the University of Utah medical school and then drove back to the house, looking at the autumn leaves falling from the trees along the road.

Thanksgiving had been difficult, and Christmas had been horrible, but today was Valentine's Day, and though this was a throwaway holiday for most people, it had always been one of Justin's favorites. I went to my closet and pulled out a shoebox full of cards. I had rubber bands around the Christmas ones, another around the birthday ones, and now I set out the batch of Valentine's Day cards.

The cards themselves were all different—a bunny looking longingly at another bunny, a cute dog holding a box of chocolates in his mouth, a handsome man holding a dove. But inside each card, the inscription was exactly the same: "Fletcher, I know I must have been valiant in the Pre-Existence or Heavenly Father wouldn't have rewarded me with you. I loved you then, I love you now, and I'll love you for the rest of eternity."

The only thing that was different from the first card and all those that followed were the additional words tagged on. "Still true."

I read each card in the stack, letting the words hit me over and over as if each card said those words for the first time.

I wished I could make a movie called *Valentine's Day*, starring Joseph Gordon-Levitt, where the lovers get to meet again for the first time in an endless loop. When he was young, Justin had looked just like the actor. "I'll look like that throughout eternity," he'd reminded me every year on his birthday.

"And I'll keep looking like Jonah Hill," I pointed out.

"That'll all be taken care of in the Resurrection." The last time he'd said it, he'd paused and then added, "I always see you now the way you'll look then."

I was forty-three and had never been much of a looker. I knew I was never going to find another husband, given the material I had to work with. But the prospect of another forty years alone was daunting. I needed to go out tonight and be with people. Though only couples would go out on a night like this, so that would probably be the worst move I could make.

I looked up movies online. *Fifty Shades of Grey* was playing. Neither Justin nor I had ever been anything but vanilla.

But our vanilla sex had kept us both interested right up till the end. Or at least till near the end. Justin had finally lost all interest in sex his last month, apologizing to me as if I cared. "That's the least of my worries," I assured him.

"I don't want us to ever lose our flame," he said.

"You'll get your flame back when you go into remission."

He shook his head. "Don't talk like that. Be honest with me."

"You'll get your flame back when you get resurrected." It was no more honest, but he accepted that one.

So what else was playing tonight? I browsed the theater website and saw my other options. There was *American Sniper*. It sounded terrible, though when I watched the news earlier today and learned that Isis had burned to death forty-five prisoners, I had to wonder where all this hatred was going to end up.

I didn't want to think about hate on Valentine's Day.

Birdman was also playing, and it was doing well in the awards circles, so it would probably be worth seeing. But it sounded too serious for my mood today.

Then there was *The Imitation Game*. That sounded serious as well, of course, about the tragic life of the gay English codebreaker from World War II. And I'd read about biographical issues with the film as well. While Turing was depicted as gay, his actual sexual relationships were glossed over in favor of one with a platonic female friend.

Still, the movie looked like my best option for the evening. I could call some of my friends, but the six people I knew were all part of three couples and would have plans of their own.

I'd lost twenty pounds during Justin's illness and thought briefly about gorging myself on vanilla ice cream tonight.

Maybe I could eat myself to death over the next few years. At that point, either I'd be reunited with Justin as he predicted, or I'd cease to exist and wouldn't be conscious of my loneliness any longer.

But it wasn't exactly loneliness I was feeling, I realized. I did have friends. And I had my work. I had my volunteer activities. I had my hobbies. My life wasn't empty. It was simply that I missed my husband.

"Please, Heavenly Father," I prayed. "Be real. Can you do that for me? Be real and take care of Justin."

I shook my head and stood up. I grabbed a sip of water from the kitchen and then headed for the door. *The Imitation Game* started in forty-five minutes. Plenty of time to get there, but I preferred waiting in the lobby over going crazy at home.

Just as I reached for the door handle, the doorbell rang. I jumped and put my hand on my heart. Peeking through the peephole, I saw a young man with a cap. I opened the door.

"Fletcher Stevens?" he asked.

"Yes?"

He handed me a bouquet of yellow daffodils, orange alstroemeria, and purple iris. The very flowers Justin used to give me every Valentine's Day. I looked at the young man in confusion as he pointed out the card attached to the bouquet.

"Who sent this?" I asked.

"Don't know," he replied. "I just deliver." He stood there a moment longer, until I realized he was waiting for a tip. I handed him the three ones I had left in my wallet. He didn't look impressed but nodded and left. I realized I'd probably been insensitive. He was out working instead of spending time with his beloved. I should have been more generous. Justin would have been generous.

I opened the card. "Fletcher, I know I must have been valiant in the Pre-existence or Heavenly Father wouldn't have rewarded me with you. I loved you then, I love you now, and I'll love you for the rest of eternity."

Oh my god.

Then I saw the two words scribbled on the back of the card. "Still true." It was all in Justin's handwriting.

Had my husband put one of our friends up to this? Written this card ahead of time, knowing this first Valentine's Day without him would be so difficult? I went to my contact list and punched Kirby's number.

"Nope, that wasn't us," he said. "But that was sure sweet of Justin."

I called Paul.

He laughed. "That sure sounds like Justin. But no, that wasn't us."

Finally, I called Hartley. He denied any participation either.

I looked at my watch. I didn't want to miss the movie, but I couldn't take my eyes away from the flowers and the card. I saw the phone number for the florist and dialed that next. I explained who I was and what had just happened.

"Oh, that," said the woman on the other end of the phone. "Yes, I remember perfectly. Your husband came in and set up a special account. He handed us a stack of signed cards and arranged to have us deliver a bouquet to you every Valentine's Day for the next thirty years."

"Th-thirty years?" I asked.

"Assuming we're still in business by then." She laughed.

I hung up the phone and sat down on my sofa with a heavy plop. I wanted to cry but I was too happy. I suddenly wanted to lose more weight so I'd be around for another thirty years. Of course, what would happen the first Valentine's Day after I turned seventy-three? Did I need to time my death that carefully?

Would the cards still mean anything if I knew they were coming and what they'd say?

Of course, that had been the case on every Valentine's Day, anyway.

And the sex had still been great though we only had a repertoire of five different activities.

I smiled. This was just like Justin. He'd always loved that scene from *The Wizard of Oz* where the Wicked Witch shakes the hourglass at Dorothy. "Fletcher, you've got just thirty years till that hourglass runs empty. Then I'll have you, my pretty."

I went over to the vase where I'd put the flowers and I sniffed the daffodils. Such a wonderful, earthy smell. My favorite.

I looked at my watch. I'd probably miss the previews, but I could still make it in time for the movie itself.

The Imitation Game. What I wanted to see was *Valentine's Day* with Joseph Gordon-Levitt.

"Please, Heavenly Father," I prayed, "let the Church still be true. Let us have an eternal marriage. Let me be with my husband again." I opened the door but then looked back inside, up toward the ceiling. "Please."

I walked outside and climbed into the car.

Looking for Nephi

"Hey, One, you ready?" I pulled our front door key out of my jeans pocket.

"Be right there, Three," Nephi said. I closed my eyes and breathed slowly. My partner was always running behind. A few minutes later, he joined me at the door. "Didn't want to forget the book," he said.

He showed me our library copy of *Rabid: A Cultural History of the World's Most Diabolical Virus*, this month's book club selection. We jumped in our Prius and headed for Cindy and Lowell's house on the other side of Pasadena.

We arrived at 7:35, just five minutes late. We knocked and walked on inside without waiting to be greeted, taking our shoes off at the door. Suzanne and Ryland were already there, seated next to each other on the sofa. Suzanne was forty-one, short and stout, with closely cropped hair that had to be helped a little to stay blond.

Ryland was a full foot taller, just over six feet, and lean. Leigh, dark-haired and slender with large breasts, was in a modern chair supported by only one leg, and Sherman, in his mid-thirties, balding and with a wispy moustache, was there in the chaise longue.

And there was a new guy, a little short at maybe 5' 5", with black hair and a goatee. He was slim, with no ass. Nephi looked at me and raised an eyebrow.

"Nephi!" Cindy said, coming into the living room from the kitchen. She was also in her early forties, like Suzanne and Ryland. "How are you?"

"Fine." I waved.

"Fine." Nephi was still appraising the new guy.

"Looks like everyone's here," Cindy concluded, "and the food's ready, so dig in."

Food was an integral part of our book club meetings on the second Friday of each month. We rotated houses, each of us hosting a few times a year. Whoever prepared dinner had to make something appealing to both omnivores and vegetarians, since the group was made up of both.

Tonight, it looked like tofu salad, with romaine lettuce, walnuts, red onions, banana peppers, and carrots, with vinaigrette dressing. There was a baguette for filler. And crangrape juice to drink. We obeyed the Word of Wisdom at these meetings.

Nephi made sure to stand in line behind the new guy, motioning with his eyes for me to look again at the guy's butt. Nephi liked small butts. He always complained that mine was too big, even though by most standards even mine was a little small. He had a bubble butt himself which he hated and I loved.

I looked at Nephi sternly, trying to wordlessly convey my disapproval. We didn't even know if the new guy was gay. No one else in the group besides us were.

We'd joined the Ex-Mormon Book Club two years previously, part of our ongoing plan to connect with more ex-Mormons. Nephi and I were dedicated fans of several of the LDS blogs: Main Street Plaza, Wheat and Tares, By Common Consent, A Marvelous Work and a Blunder, Ex-Mormon Mavens, Life after Mormonism, and Ward Gossip.

We also subscribed to q-saints, a gay Mormon email group, and we read *Sunstone* magazine and *Dialogue* regularly. When we'd heard about this book club so close to home, we jumped at the chance to join.

"I'm Nephi," I said to the new guy, offering my hand after he sat down with his plate.

"Jahanzeb," he replied, shaking my hand with enthusiasm. Must still be active in the Church.

"And I'm Nephi, too," my partner said, nudging me aside. "Well, really, Nephi One. And this is Nephi Three." He pointed to me. "People just call us One and Three when we're together. Cuts down on the confusion."

Jahanzeb frowned. "Why not One and Two?" he asked, stabbing a bit of walnut with his fork.

Ryland held up his hand. "Let me," he said. "They want to be the Three Nephites, but there's only two of them so far. And they left the blank space in the middle so they'd never forget they weren't complete."

Jahanzeb stopped with the walnut halfway to his mouth. "You aren't serious?"

"Yes," I said. "There's no reason the Three Nephites have to all be named Nephi, but since Nephi and I both share the name, we thought it would be nice."

Jahanzeb slowly continued bringing the walnut closer to his mouth.

"Moroni or Alma or Ammon would do just fine, of course, but it should really be a scriptural name," Nephi said.

"So where are you from?" Leigh asked, pointing at Jahanzeb with her fork.

It was hard to know when the question was rude or when it demonstrated genuine interest. Since most of the group had lived in other countries during our mission days, we had at least some sense of a global community. I hoped Jahanzeb didn't take offense.

"Afghanistan." He took another bite of salad. Nephi and I sat down in the chairs on either side of him. I prayed the young man wouldn't drop a walnut on his pants because I knew my partner would reach over to brush it off.

That would be rude.

"There can't possibly be many Mormons there," Sherman said.

"I converted when I came to America six years ago," he explained. "Then went on a mission two years later to Switzerland." He looked to be in his mid-twenties, I noted, maybe five or six years younger than Nephi and I.

"You'd never consider legally changing your name?" Nephi asked, a slice of baguette in his hand.

"To Nephi?" Jahanzeb laughed. "You must be crazy. I'm *leaving* the Church. I certainly don't want a Mormon name *now*."

"What made you decide to leave?" I asked.

He shrugged. "When I realized that DNA studies proved there was no link between Native Americans and Jews."

"Ah." Lowell joined us after setting out the last of the food. He was thirty-nine, a few years younger than his wife, Cindy. He turned to Ryland. "How about you guys? When did you know you were going to leave the Church?"

It wasn't as if we hadn't all shared these details with one another, but we repeated them each time a new member joined the group. It seemed impossible for newbies to move forward until the question was answered, relevant and irrelevant at the same time.

Though I noted Jahanzeb wasn't the one who asked.

Ryland looked at Suzanne and motioned for her to answer first. She shook her head, pointing to her mouth, busy chewing, and motioned back for Ryland to respond. "When I learned that blacks could hold the priesthood in the early Church, and then it was taken away."

Suzanne had finished her mouthful by now and added, "I knew when I learned how many prominent members of the early Church owned slaves. I'd always been taught the Church was anti-slavery."

Ryland and Suzanne both looked white, but they'd told us before they each had one black grandparent. It seemed an odd coincidence, but then Nephi and I were in no position to scoff at coincidences.

"I knew I was going to leave the Church when I realized we were never going to give the priesthood to women," Lowell said.

"And I knew it when I realized I didn't even like the priesthood," said Cindy, "and I didn't want it for either myself or my husband." She put her hand on Lowell's shoulder.

"What about you guys?" Lowell asked, pointing to Leigh and Sherman. They weren't a couple, Leigh married to a non-Mormon and Sherman perhaps a tad too nerdy to hook up with anyone.

"The Mountain Meadows Massacre did it for me." Leigh pointed at an oil painting of western scenery on the wall, though it wasn't Mountain Meadows.

Sherman took a sip of his juice and looked thoughtful. "I suppose I knew when I finished reading *Lord of the Rings* for the first time and realized it was better as scripture than either the Book of Mormon *or* the Bible."

Everyone laughed.

"And the Nephis?" Jahanzeb asked.

Hmm, he did ask about *us*.

"I knew when I left for my mission," Nephi said. "I was going to Finland, to Helsinki, and the abbreviation for the airport there is HEL. I was on Flight 666, flying out of Salt Lake on Friday the 13th, going to HEL.”

Everyone laughed again.

“I knew the moment I met Nephi at a Singles dance,” I said. “We kept looking at each other while we were dancing with girls, and at the end of the evening, he asked me to come over to his place.”

“You slut.” Leigh wagged a finger at Nephi.

“Well, I went,” I said, “so I guess I’m a slut, too.”

“Slut One and Slut Two,” said Lowell.

“I think we’ll stick with Nephi One and Nephi Three.”

“You guys met at a Singles dance?” Jahanzeb scrunched up his nose. So cute. “Maybe I should keep going to church.”

“So you’re gay, too?” Nephi asked. “I *knew* it!”

“Don’t get any ideas,” he said. “I’m not into polygamy.”

“Polyandry,” Nephi corrected.

“Are you a top or a bottom?” asked Nephi. “I hope you’re a bottom.”

“Uh, guys,” said Cindy, “we’re here to discuss the book.”

“First we have to select the book for the meeting two months from now,” Lowell reminded us.

“Who brought books?” asked Suzanne.

“I did,” said Leigh.

"What's our topic for next time?" Sherman asked.

Lowell consulted a piece of paper. "It's Mormon-Other-Other-Mormon-Other-Other. What Mormon books do you have for us, Leigh?"

She pulled out a folder and began handing out synopses and reviews. "I brought *Hippie Boy* from Ingrid Ricks. It's only marginally Mormon, but it made the *New York Times* bestseller list, about her life growing up in a dysfunctional Mormon family. Then there's *Following the Liahona* by Jeff Salinas, about an elder who gets lost in St. Petersburg and ends up in the bed of a Russian Orthodox priest. There's *Latter-Day Ain'ts* and *Faith-Promoting Rumors*, both collections of short stories."

"Well, I knew what I was getting into," Jahanzeb said.

We read the pages Leigh passed around. It was difficult coming up with Mormon books worth reading. We certainly had no intention of buying from Deseret Book. Signature Books had some good titles, but a lot of them were heavily academic, and we really just wanted to have fun.

Nephi and I had our own karaoke machine at home. I wondered what songs Jahanzeb might want us to program into it.

We voted, and the winner for the book we'd be discussing in two more months was *Following the Liahona.* The truth was that most of the other books we'd been presented with tonight would probably show up again in a few months the next time a Mormon book had to be picked. There weren't so many that we could discard three or four at a time and never come back to them again. But that was okay. Most of the others had sounded good, too.

Then came time to talk about *Rabid.* Cindy turned on a recording of a dog growling softly in the background. "It was fascinating to see how people could be persuaded to believe in werewolves just by watching a real person become infected with rabies," she observed. "I can't believe all the wild things a person will believe."

"I don't believe you," Nephi quipped.

"I didn't get that far into the book," Ryland said.

"That was in the introduction." Leigh wagged her finger at him.

"What I find interesting," I said, "is to see how we react so differently to the same material."

"Some of us have taste."

"Some of us taste good."

"Taste this."

"Jahanzeb, how are you liking things so far?"

"It's worth coming back," he replied, a bit too slowly. "Can I bring the book choices next month?"

"With that ringing endorsement? Sure."

Jahanzeb looked as if he thought the evening was over, but it was only 8:45. We were still just getting started. Sherman talked about the latest episode of *The Big Bang Theory*, Lowell talked about being chewed out by his boss in front of his coworkers, and Suzanne mentioned the two Colorado politicians who'd just been recalled because they voted for some tiny measure toward gun regulation.

Ryland brought up the President wanting to bomb Syria, and we talked about whether we believed Armageddon would truly start one day in the Middle East.

I'd never felt an automatic bond with other Mormons just because we were Mormon, but somehow, I did feel that connection with many ex-Mormons.

When I'd been with other Mormons at church, I'd always felt a wall between us. I knew that deep down, none of them would like me if they knew my secret. I couldn't even vote for a pro-choice candidate without looking over my shoulder and wondering if I was going to be reported to the bishop. Most Mormons accepted NSA spying with no qualms because it was already the norm in their religious practice.

"I think the West underestimates the turmoil in Muslim countries," Jahanzeb said. "They certainly don't understand the complexity."

Nephi caught my attention and tapped lightly on his cheek, tilting his head ever so slightly toward Jahanzeb. I looked more closely at the young man. He had a dimple in his left cheek. I looked back at Nephi. He was smiling.

So much for understanding complexity.

"I was watching *Your Bleeped Up Brain* the other day," Cindy said, "and they showed that people were more likely to believe utter nonsense if it was said by an attractive person.

Not every missionary is attractive, but they *are* young, and that makes them automatically attractive to some people."

"I resent that implication." Nephi made a show of sucking in his gut. He was all of five pounds overweight.

I noticed Jahanzeb looking briefly at Nephi's stomach. I couldn't quite tell if his eyes focused any lower.

"We're also quicker to believe things if they're told to us by someone who looks authoritative in a business suit," Cindy continued.

"Sounds like Sacrament meeting," said Nephi.

"And stake conference," said Lowell.

"And General Conference," said Ryland.

"And those darn missionaries," said Jahanzeb. He closed his eyes with a wistful expression.

Nephi was right about Jahanzeb, I thought. He was adorable. We'd have to ask him out and try to become better friends, even if he wasn't the missing piece in our relationship puzzle. Our fifth anniversary was coming up, and we were feeling the emptiness of our absent partner more than usual. Odd how Nephi and I shared not only our name but from the start, we'd both fantasized about a permanent three-way relationship.

We'd put our profiles up on every gay dating website, explaining our desire and its Mormon specifications. We'd attended Affirmation conferences and Sunstone symposia looking for another gay Nephi. I was sure most people thought we were kooks. Perhaps we were.

It was hard to imagine anyone damaged by religion not carrying excess baggage. You'd think the heavy emotional load would make us all emotionally stronger.

"Brigham Young believed people lived on the moon."

"He also taught that God slipped Mary a roofie and then raped her."

"Righteously, of course."

"If a god does it, it's not illegal!" Lowell said, attempting a barely recognizable Nixon impression.

"An early U.S. president believed the Earth was hollow and mole people lived inside," said Cindy, "because a successful military man told him. I don't suppose we can really blame Mormons for believing what they do. It's just a result of the way human brains work."

Jahanzeb's eyes were glowing. I was glad he was having a good time. I also noticed that Nephi's eyes glowed as he looked at Jahanzeb.

I sensed some roleplay tonight after we got home.

I wondered if it would be inappropriate to pull the young man aside before we left and ask him how to say a couple of sexy things in…

What language did they speak in Afghanistan? Persian? Arabic? Urdu?

I was way too ignorant.

"I saw a show explaining how aliens might take over the Earth," Sherman said. "They might use telepathy and mind control. They could make us see things that weren't there, or feel fear for no apparent reason, things like that."

"So you think aliens are behind religion?" Jahanzeb asked.

Sherman shrugged. "I was thinking maybe God himself is an alien, not really a god. Just some other powerful species from another planet, with the power to manipulate us in all these ways."

"It's a shame you're no longer an active member of the Church," I said. "I'd love to hear you give a talk like that in Sacrament meeting."

"*I* believe in something ridiculous," Nephi said abruptly.

"What's that?" asked Leigh.

"I believe in reincarnation. I believe Nephi and I are the reincarnation of two of the Three Nephites."

Everyone laughed until they saw he looked serious. I'd already heard this from him before and wasn't on the same page, but there was no requirement partners agree on everything.

"But how can you be their reincarnation?" Suzanne asked. "The whole point of that story is they never died."

"And Mormons don't believe in reincarnation anyway," Ryland added.

"I'm not Mormon anymore."

"But you still believe in the Three Nephites?" asked Jahanzeb.

"It's our bleeped up brain," Cindy said. "Not even 'enlightened' people can escape biology."

"I have to admit, I still believe in the idea of eternal progression."

"I still believe in eternal existence. That we existed even before we were born."

"And I still believe in Jesus Christ."

"Maybe we're acting stuffy when we laugh at Mormons," Cindy said. "We're really a lot more like them than we are different."

"We're fucked up, too," I conceded. "But there *is* a difference. We've managed to focus on justice and equality despite our limitations. We manage to see just a *little* bit farther."

Though even that was a rationalization so we could feel good about ourselves.

The talk began to die down, and finally, around 10:00, Leigh stood and announced it was time to leave. At that point, almost everyone else stood up, too. We thanked Cindy and Lowell for hosting, and then Nephi and I followed Jahanzeb out to his car. After he unlocked his door, he turned back to us.

"I'm a bottom," he said.

Nephi made a motion like he was blasting a horn in an eighteen-wheeler. "Yes!"

"And I'm a top, too," he added.

"Yes!" I said.

Jahanzeb laughed and held out his hand. "Give me your phone number, and we'll see about getting together tomorrow evening."

Nephi quickly wrote his number on a card he had in his pocket.

"I can't promise any Book of Mormon fantasies," he went on. "Though I did always wonder about the relationship between Joseph Smith, Sidney Ridgon, and Martin Harris."

We laughed.

"I may be more comfortable being Slut Three than Nephi Two."

"We'll ask the aliens to change your mind," Nephi assured him.

"Or at least wear authoritative suits when you show up at our place."

"Now that could work." Jahanzeb nodded. "I still have my missionary nametag."

He smiled again, we all hugged, and then he climbed into his car and drove off. Maybe we *were* fucked up, I thought, as humans, as Mormons, and especially as ex-Mormons. Nephi and I looked at each other, kissed, and headed for our car. We drove home slowly with the windows down, enjoying the cool night air, quiet as we reflected on the evening.

Back at our apartment, I went to the computer and ordered *Following the Liahona*. Then Nephi and I stripped down to our garments, gave each other a blow job through the slits in front, and slid under the covers to go to sleep.

Your Mission, If You Choose to Accept It

"Uh, I don't feel so good." Elder Marks put his hand on his stomach. "Do you mind if I use your bathroom?"

Antonio motioned toward the hallway leading deeper into the apartment so my companion could find relief. There was a large crack in the wall from the earthquake last November. Over three thousand people in Campania and Basilicata had been killed on that dreadful day, but in some ways 1980 was the year of my birth. I felt far more alive out here in Italy than I had back in Scottsdale.

Every day was an adventure, stopping people on the streets, knocking on the doors of strangers, eating dinner with new contacts. We were eating spaghetti alle vongole tonight, something I'd never had before. Elder Marks stood up from the table with his hand still on his stomach and hurried down the hall. Antonio turned to me and grinned. How embarrassing for Elder Marks.

"Anziano," Antonio began. "No—Giuseppe—we have to talk quickly."

My name was Joseph Lucas, but as a Mormon missionary, I was simply called Elder Lucas for the two years I was on my mission. Yet it thrilled me to hear Antonio use the Italian version, like a code name. I felt sophisticated speaking a second language. In some ways, I even felt like a spy, living outwardly as a dedicated Latter-day Saint while leading a secret life underneath that I hid from everyone, from my companions, the mission leaders, and especially the investigators I was trying to inspire.

I fantasized about meeting someone who knew my secret, someone who could then call me on another, better assignment. But of course I would never really leave my mission. Or the Church, for that matter. It was just a fantasy I let myself dream, to add another layer of sophistication to my life. A shy reader addicted to Ian Fleming led a pretty pathetic existence, especially now that Ian Fleming was forbidden reading material.

No movies allowed, either. When Antonio called me Giuseppe, it felt like we were sharing a secret. "Sí," I replied, "che c'é?" We were of course speaking Italian throughout the entire meal. I'd been out fourteen months, the last four here in Napoli, and Elder Marks had been out five since leaving the Missionary Training Center. Even he could muddle through a conversation.

"Giuseppe, I put something in your companion's food to make him sick."

"What?"

"There was no other way to speak to you alone. You guys are always together."

"It's the mission rule. So we don't stray."

Antonio closed his eyes. "That's exactly what I want to talk to you about." He paused. Sometimes, there was a look about him that made me wonder if he led a double life, too.

Elder Marks and I had tracted him out almost five weeks earlier. He was twenty-two and worked as a shoe salesman.

At least, that was his cover, I allowed. We'd taught him all our lessons, plus several invented ones to justify our visits. He'd only come out to church once and wouldn't commit to baptism, so this was going to be our last evening with him. Besides, when I'd called earlier to make an appointment to say goodbye, I'd told him I was being transferred tomorrow back up to Rome where I'd started.

"Giuseppe, I want you to move in with me."

I stared at Antonio in surprise. We'd always gotten along well. I liked him and had told him so. Elder Marks and I had even invited him to go to the Capodimonte museum with us one P-Day. I'd also told him I'd thought of studying Italian more thoroughly after I finished my mission, that I might even move here permanently, but I certainly couldn't get a roommate right now.

I looked at him suspiciously. It seemed a strange invitation. Was he truly leading a secret life? Perhaps he was asking me to go undercover with him.

Undercover? I was such an idiot. Sometimes, when I spent too much time daydreaming, it took me a minute to recognize reality again. I'd read somewhere that method actors could have similar problems.

Of course, Antonio *had* slipped something into the food. That was something Peter Graves on *Mission: Impossible* might have done.

"What are you talking about?" I set my fork down. "I still have ten months left." Still, to have the possibility of housing as soon as I was ready for civilian life again was intoxicating. I wanted to keep this feeling of sophistication. Having a secret life in Scottsdale would feel empty. If I had to have a secret life, I wanted to do it in this exotic country. And while Rome was cleaner than Naples, it was the people of Naples I really loved. So open and friendly, like Antonio. His olive skin promised…something.

Antonio reached over and put his hand on mine. That was another reason I loved Italy. Men could touch each other, show affection. I knew I could never really *be* with another man the way I wanted, but this was the next best thing. I'd insisted on continuing these meetings with Antonio for just that reason, even though Elder Marks had said three visits ago we should dump him.

"I want you to move in right now. I can't wait ten months."

"But you only have one bedroom," I replied. "Even if I did want to be roommates, we'd have to find another apartment."

"We only need one bed," Antonio said. I felt my hand trembling underneath his.

I stared at him, the way people looked at Barbara Bain taking off her latex mask and revealing her true face underneath. "Tu sei…" I faltered. "Tu sei…"

"Un finocchio. Sí."

"Flip," I said in English.

"What?"

I heard a loud groan come from the back of the apartment. "Is he going to be okay?" I asked.

"Probably."

"Antonio, do you know what you're asking me?"

He nodded. "I've been meaning to tell you for a while now, but I was afraid you'd stop coming over. But since you're leaving anyway, I figured I didn't have anything to lose."

"But I hardly know you," I protested. I didn't even ask how he could tell I was gay, too. I was always amazed no one had suspected yet, constantly afraid of being found out. I felt I was meeting up with an ally in enemy territory.

"How long does it take to know you're in love?" Antonio took my hand and led me from the small kitchen table over to the sofa. It was covered in tan fabric that was fraying at the edges.

He sat down and pulled me onto the cushion beside him. Now he held both my hands in his lap. "You're handsome," he went on, "you speak Italian better than I do, and I've seen the way you look at me. You want me, too. Don't deny it."

I shook my head. While all this was thrilling to hear, the truth was we *weren't* spies. We were ordinary people. And I was Mormon. What he was asking was impossible. "But we don't have anything in common," I said. "All I know is that you like calcio and I don't. Look at those posters on your wall." I nodded toward the two huge photographs of prominent Italian soccer stars tacked to his living room wall. One of them covered half of another crack.

"I don't give a damn about soccer," he returned. "Those guys are up there because they're hot. But I'll take them down for you."

The world was reeling. I felt dizzy. Was it another earthquake? I wondered if Antonio had slipped something into my food as well. Maybe he wasn't a spy for any Earthly country, but he must certainly be an agent of the Adversary. I heard an agonized grunt from down the hall. Were we both about to be murdered? Degenerates could do anything.

I looked at Antonio, who was staring at me intently. Then I looked at my hands in his lap. Where they shouldn't be. He saw my glance and pressed down on my hands. I felt…

Oh my heck.

"Giuseppe, I know what I'm asking. It's hard for me, too. My family doesn't know, but they will if you move in. I'm willing to risk people finding out my secret. For true love. Aren't you willing to risk anything?"

"But I have the true church," I said. "You're not risking the same thing. I'm risking *everything*." Even I could tell I sounded like an ass. Why would this guy even want me in the first place? I was no Sean Connery. Or George Lazenby, for that matter.

Antonio leaned over, his face coming nearer and nearer. I knew what he was about to do. I should get up, I thought. I should run outside, even if it meant leaving my companion to fend for himself. I should…

He kissed me. I'd never even kissed a girl before and didn't know what to expect. After only a few seconds, the first thought that popped into my head was, "So *this* is what everyone is always talking about." It was wonderful.

This was the kind of thing James Bond did.

The kiss lasted a long time. Or at least it felt like it did. But all too soon, Antonio was pulling his head back. "I know you know," was all he said.

I pulled my hands out of his lap and turned to face a soccer player with firm, hairy legs. "This is essentially the first date I've ever had in my life," I said. The two girls I'd dated a handful of times each certainly didn't count. They'd been the ones to break it off with me when it became clear there was no chemistry. "You can't expect me to marry someone after only one date." This wasn't a game, even if I did feel like I was playing chess with Kronsteen.

"That's pretty much what Elder Marks intends to do after he goes home, isn't it?" Antonio asked with a grin.

"It's…it's not the same."

Antonio sighed. "Giuseppe, we don't have much time." He looked down the hallway, which was silent now. "Please, when you leave your apartment tomorrow, don't go to the train station. Come here instead."

"Non posso," I said, hardly able to form the words. "I can't." I had always known I'd have to forego love to remain a good Mormon and reach the Celestial Kingdom. But now I knew it in a way I never had before. It was like the difference in *saying* you knew the Church was true, and actually *knowing* it.

Testimonies sucked.

I looked down at Antonio's crotch.

I wanted to be James Bond.

"You can teach English to make a few dollars until you find a regular job. I know it's hard to get work in Naples. And it'll be worse since you're American. We'll be poor. But it'll work out. You'll see. Have faith. You can have faith, can't you?"

"Antonio…" How could I have faith in sin? This wasn't some childish game, I reminded myself again.

Antonio grabbed my face with his hands. "Answer me this—do you love me?"

I looked at him and hesitated.

"Yes or no?"

"Yes," I said. "Yes." He smiled, and my heart melted. I would give away nuclear secrets for that smile.

But I wouldn't give up the Celestial Kingdom for it.

We heard the door to the bathroom opening. Antonio dug into his pants quickly. "Here's a key. I have to work tomorrow, but I want to see you here when I come home." He slipped the key into my hand, and I shoved it in my pocket.

Why didn't I throw it on the floor?

"Elder Marks, are you feeling better?" Antonio asked, sounding sincere. Who could believe anything a guy like that said? He was an agent of Kaos. But a serious one. He wanted to destroy me, and then he'd kick me out on the street and laugh. The war between heaven and hell was a Cold War, and I didn't want to end up a prisoner in some god-forsaken cell.

"Anziano," Elder Marks panted, "we've got to go home." We picked up our scriptures and headed for the door.

"No prayer?" Antonio asked, a little sardonically.

Elder Marks flung open the door and hurried out. We'd have a fifteen minute wait for the bus, and then another fifteen minute trip back to our neighborhood. I hoped we'd make it. We stood underneath the streetlamp, Elder Marks with one hand on his stomach. Would Antonio do something like that to *me* one day?

What if we had an argument? What if he wanted to break up? He was a classic villain. Worse than Blofeld. Even if he weren't asking the most outrageous sacrifice from me to begin with, he was in no way the kind of guy I could ever trust with my life.

And I didn't want to live with *any* guy. I wanted to marry a pure woman in the temple and have lots of happy children. Why was I entertaining his suggestion even for the merest second? It was preposterous. I was a good boy. And I was going to stay a good boy forever. I wasn't going to lead a secret life. I was a Mormon, and I was going to live openly and honestly.

"I don't feel so good."

"Hang in there, Elder. We'll be home soon."

Thankfully, the bus came only a moment later, and traffic was lighter than usual, so we were home within a few minutes. Heavenly Father looked out for his own. And punished traitors. There would probably be another earthquake in Naples if I tried to see Antonio again. In fact, I should have dusted my shoes off when we left his apartment.

That kind of curse was not to be cast lightly, but if anything warranted it, this did. Dusting one's shoes wasn't a missile from a car, or a knife from a shoe sole. It was a real weapon, a weapon of the Spirit. I had to focus on reality before my delusions destroyed me.

We were back in our apartment by 8:15, way too early. If we didn't get caught by the district leader, though, we could say we got in an hour later. Elder Marks headed straight for the bathroom, and I went to our room. I'd packed my extra suit, my shirts and garments, my second pair of shoes, my ties, and my journal and tape recorder already.

I packed my color-coded colloqui and my copies of *La grande apostasia* and *Il miracolo del perdono* now. I would wear the same shirt tomorrow morning, as there was no need to be 100% fresh to spend the day transferring. Missionaries traveled light. Like spies.

I bit my lip for continuing the fantasy, even when I knew it was long past time to stop.

I was *trying* to trick myself into staying. Fantasizing was a sin.

Everything I owned was in the two suitcases. Everything I owned except my soul. And I did still own that. But I'd lose it forever tomorrow if I did what Antonio asked.

And yet…and yet…I'd been praying for this exact opportunity ever since I could remember. I loved Italy. I loved Italian men. I loved the language, the food, the music. The words to a Claudio Baglioni song kept repeating in my mind. And I wanted that secret life. But I loved my mission, too. I was one of the few missionaries who didn't bellyache every night. I *enjoyed* spreading the gospel.

Still, the whole point of having the gospel was to create great families. Here I had the chance to create the only family that would ever make me happy, and I was throwing it away.

But wickedness never was happiness.

"You okay?" Elder Marks trudged wearily into the bedroom. "You don't look so good, either."

"Maybe we ought to get to bed before the others come home."

"I'm sorry I made you leave early. I know you liked Antonio."

"It's okay."

"Well, you have to get moving as soon as you wake up tomorrow, anyway, so maybe we *had* better hit the sack."

"Shall I offer the companion prayer?" I asked.

"Thanks." We knelt together in the middle of the room while I prayed, and then I turned off the light and we both climbed into our cots wearing just our garments. I'd never be able to wear garments again if I went to see Antonio. I *liked* my garments. It was a blessing when even your underwear reminded you to think of God.

It was like having a secret chip implanted in your arm.

Stop it, Joseph, I told myself. Just stop it.

Giuseppe sounded so much nicer than Joseph.

I could be a *real* boy.

If I went to Antonio's tomorrow, 1981 would be my death date. I was only twenty. That was too young. I didn't want to die a spiritual death. I didn't want to end up in Outer Darkness with Satan. Even Antonio admitted he'd never lived with another guy before. We'd be sure to blow it even if we tried to make it work. I'd lose out on eternal life and still end up with nothing here on Earth.

No fool would make such a decision.

I needed to be an adult. I was no longer a teenager watching action movies with other kids. Reading books that only fulfilled the writer's juvenile dreams.

I'd take the first bus that came by in the morning and head straight for the train station before I had a chance to sin. You had to know your own weaknesses and work around them. That's what real people did. Not some stupid fantasy figure. Heavenly Father would note this tremendous sacrifice and bless me. I might even become a zone leader. My family would be proud of me, instead of wishing I was dead.

I closed my eyes and tried to clear the sin out of my brain. I slept fitfully, the single blanket somehow not enough, even though it was only early September.

Making the right decision was supposed to bring peace of mind.

I said goodbye to the other elders at 7:00 the following morning and carried my two heavy suitcases to the bus stop alone. I thought about making a quick stop by Antonio's just to brush the dust from my shoes. Perhaps Heavenly Father would make Vesuvius blow this time.

Instead, I cleared out a couple of drawers and put away my things, changing into the jeans I usually only wore on Preparation Day, taking off my garments and going without. I swept the floor and washed some dishes from last night that were still in the sink.

The ordinary had never felt so exotic. I straightened some books on Antonio's scratched bookcase and dusted his worn dresser. And by late afternoon I had a fresh salad on the table, with sugo cooking on the stove, when not *The Spy Who Loved Me* but the man I loved came home.

Books by Johnny Townsend

Thanks for reading! If you enjoyed this book, could you please take a few minutes to write a review online? Reviews are helpful both to me as an author and to other readers, so we'd all sincerely appreciate your writing one! And if you did enjoy the book, here are some others I've written you might want to look up:

Mormon Underwear

Zombies for Jesus

A Gay Mormon Missionary in Pompeii

The Golem of Rabbi Loew

Escape from Zion

Marginal Mormons

Gay Gaslighting

Going-Out-Of-Religion Sale

Sins of the Saints

Gayrabian Nights

Missionaries Make the Best Companions

Invasion of the Spirit Snatchers

Mormon Misfits

The Washing of Brains

A Mormon Motive for Murder

The Moat around Zion

The Last Days Linger

The Mysterious Madness of Mormons

Human Compassion for Beginners

Breaking the Promise of the Promised Land

I Will, Through the Veil

Am I My Planet's Keeper?

Have Your Cum and Eat It, Too

Strangers with Benefits

Constructing Equity

Wake Up and Smell the Missionaries

Racism by Proxy

Orgy at the STD Clinic

Life Is Better with Love

Please Evacuate

Recommended Daily Humanity

The Camper Killings

Kinky Quilts: Patchwork Designs for Gay Men

Inferno in the French Quarter: The UpStairs Lounge Fire

Latter-Gay Saints: An Anthology of Gay Mormon Fiction (co-editor)

Available from your favorite online or neighborhood bookstore.

Wondering what some of those other books are about? Read on!

Invasion of the Spirit Snatchers

During the Apocalypse, a group of Mormon survivors in Hurricane, Utah gather in the home of the Relief Society president, telling stories to pass the time as they ration their food storage and await the Second

Coming. But this is no ordinary group of Mormons—or perhaps it is. They are the faithful, feminist, gay, apostate, and repentant, all working together to help each other through the darkest days any of them have yet seen.

Gayrabian Nights

Gayrabian Nights is a twist on the well-known classic, *1001 Arabian Nights*, in which Scheherazade, under the threat of death if she ceases to captivate King Shahryar's attention, enchants him through a series of mysterious, adventurous, and romantic tales.

In this variation, a male escort, invited to the hotel room of a closeted, homophobic Mormon senator, learns that the man is poised to vote on a piece of anti-gay legislation the following morning. To prevent him from sleeping, so that the exhausted senator will miss casting his vote on the Senate floor, the escort entertains him with stories of homophobia, celibacy, mixed orientation marriages, reparative therapy, coming out, first love, gay marriage, and long-term successful gay relationships. The escort crafts the stories to give the senator a crash course in gay culture and sensibilities, hoping to bring the man closer to accepting his own sexual orientation.

Inferno in the French Quarter: The UpStairs Lounge Fire

On Gay Pride Day in 1973, someone set the entrance to a French Quarter gay bar on fire. In the terrible inferno that followed, thirty-two people lost their lives, including a third of the local congregation of the Metropolitan Community Church, their pastor burning to death halfway out a second-story window as he tried to claw his way to freedom. A mother who'd gone to the bar with her two gay sons died alongside them.

A man who'd helped his friend escape first was found dead near the fire escape. Two children waited outside a movie theater across town for a father and step-father who would never pick them up. During this era of rampant homophobia, several families refused to claim the bodies, and many churches refused to bury the dead.

Author Johnny Townsend pored through old records and tracked down survivors of the fire as well as relatives and friends of those killed to compile this fascinating account of a forgotten moment in gay history.

A Gay Mormon Missionary in Pompeii

What is a gay Mormon missionary doing in Italy? He is trying to save his own soul as well as the souls of others. In these tales chronicling the two-year mission of Robert Anderson, we see a young man tormented by his inability to be the man the Church says he should be. In addition to his personal hell, Anderson faces a major earthquake, organized crime, a serious bus accident, and much more. He copes with horrendous mission leaders and his own suicidal tendencies. But one day, he meets another missionary who loves him, and his world changes forever.

Missionaries Make the Best Companions

What lies behind the freshly scrubbed façades of the Mormon missionaries we see about town? In these stories, an ex-Mormon tries to seduce a faithful elder by showing him increasingly suggestive movies. A sister missionary fulfills her community service requirement by babysitting for a prostitute. Two elders break their mission rules by venturing into the forbidden French Quarter. A senior missionary couple try to reactivate lapsed members while their own family falls apart back home. A young man hopes that serving a second full-time mission will lead him up the Church hierarchy. Two bored missionaries decide to make a little extra money moonlighting in a male stripper club. Two frustrated elders find an acceptable way to masturbate—by donating to a Fertility Clinic. A lonely man searches for the favorite companion he hasn't seen in thirty years.

The Golem of Rabbi Loew

Jacob and Esau Cohen are the closest of brothers. In fact, they're lovers. A doctor tries to combine canine genes with those of Jews, to improve their chances of surviving a hostile world. A Talmudic scholar dates an escort. A scientist tries to develop the "God spot" in the brains of his patients in order to create a messiah. The Golem of Prague is really Rabbi Loew's secret lover. While some of the Jews in Townsend's book are Orthodox, this collection of Jewish stories most certainly is not.

Am I My Planet's Keeper?

Global Warming. Climate Change. Climate Crisis. Climate Emergency. Whatever label we use, we are facing one of the greatest challenges to the survival of life as we know it.

But while addressing greenhouse gases is perhaps our most urgent need, it's not our only task. We must also address toxic waste, pollution, habitat destruction, and our other contributions to the world's sixth mass extinction event.

In order to do that, we must simultaneously address the unmet human needs that keep us distracted from deeper engagement in stabilizing our climate: moderating economic inequality, guaranteeing healthcare to all, and ensuring education for everyone.

And to accomplish *that*, we must unite to combat the monied forces that use fear, prejudice, and misinformation to manipulate us.

It's a daunting task. But success is our only option.

Wake Up and Smell the Missionaries

Two Mormon missionaries in Italy discover they share the same rare ability—both can emit pheromones on demand. At first, they playfully compete in the hills of Frascati to see who can tempt "investigators" most. But soon they're targeting each other non-stop.

Can two immature young men learn to control their "superpower" to live a normal life…and develop genuine love? Even as their relationship is threatened by the attentions of another man?

They seem just on the verge of success when a massive earthquake leaves them trapped under the rubble of their apartment in Castellammare.

With night falling and temperatures dropping, can they dig themselves out in time to save themselves? And will their injuries destroy the ability that brought them together in the first place?

Orgy at the STD Clinic

Todd Tillotson is struggling to move on after his husband is killed in a hit and run attack a year earlier during a Black Lives Matter protest in Seattle.

In this novel set entirely on public transportation, we watch as Todd, isolated throughout the pandemic, battles desperation in his attempt to safely reconnect with the world.

Will he find love again, even casual friendship, or will he simply end up another crazy old man on the bus?

Things don't look good until a man whose face he can't even see sits down beside him despite the raging variants.

And asks him a question that will change his life.

Please Evacuate

A gay, partygoing New Yorker unconcerned about the future or the unsustainability of capitalism is hit by a truck and thrust into a straight man's body half a continent away. As Hunter tries to figure out what's happening, he's caught up in another disaster, a wildfire sweeping through a Colorado community, the flames overtaking him and several schoolchildren as they flee.

When he awakens, Hunter finds himself in the body of yet another man, this time in northern Italy, a former missionary about to marry a young Mormon woman. Still piecing together this new reality, and beginning to embrace his latest identity, Hunter fights for his life in a devastating flash flood along with his wife *and* his new husband.

He's an aging worker in drought-stricken Texas, a nurse at an assisted living facility in the direct path of a hurricane, an advocate for the unhoused during a freak Seattle blizzard.

We watch as Hunter is plunged into life after life, finally recognizing the futility of only looking out for #1 and understanding the part he must play in addressing the global climate crisis…if he ever gets another chance.

Recommended Daily Humanity

A checklist of human rights must include basic housing, universal healthcare, equitable funding for public schools, and tuition-free college and vocational training.

In addition to the basics, though, we need much more to fully thrive. Subsidized childcare, universal pre-K, a universal basic income, subsidized high-speed internet, net neutrality, fare-free public transit (plus *more* public transit), and medically assisted death for the terminally ill who want it.

None of this will matter, though, if we neglect to address the rapidly worsening climate crisis.

Sound expensive? It is.

But not as expensive as refusing to implement these changes. The cost of climate disasters each year has grown to staggering figures. And the cost of social and political upheaval from not meeting the needs of suffering workers, families, and individuals may surpass even that.

It's best we understand that the vast sums required to enact meaningful change are an investment which will pay off not only in some indeterminate future but in fact almost immediately. And without these adjustments to our lifestyles and values, there may very well not be a future capable of sustaining freedom and democracy…or even civilization itself.

The Camper Killings

When a homeless man is found murdered a few blocks from Morgan Beylerian's house in south Seattle, everyone seems to consider the body just so much additional trash to be cleared from the neighborhood. But Morgan liked the guy. They used to chat when Morgan brought Nick groceries once a week.

And the brutal way the man was killed reminds Morgan of their shared Mormon heritage, back when the faithful agreed to have their throats slit if they ever revealed temple secrets.

Did Nick's former wife take action when her ex-husband refused to grant a temple divorce? Did his murder have something to do with the public accusations that brought an end to his promising career?

Morgan does his best to investigate when no one else seems to care, but it isn't easy as a man living paycheck to paycheck himself, only able to pursue his investigation via public transit.

As he continues his search for the killer, Morgan's friends withdraw and his husband threatens to leave. When another homeless man is killed and Morgan is accused of the crime, things look even bleaker.

But his troubles aren't over yet.

Will Morgan find the killer before the killer finds him?

What Readers Have Said

Townsend's stories are "a gay *Portnoy's Complaint* of Mormonism. Salacious, sweet, sad, insightful, insulting, religiously ethnic, quirky-faithful, and funny."

D. Michael Quinn, author of *The Mormon Hierarchy: Origins of Power*

"Told from a believably conversational first-person perspective, [*A Gay Mormon Missionary in Pompeii*'s] novelistic focus on Anderson's journey to thoughtful self-acceptance allows for greater character development than often seen in short stories, which makes this well-paced work rich and satisfying, and one of Townsend's strongest. An extremely important contribution to the field of Mormon fiction." Named to Kirkus Reviews' Best of 2011.

Kirkus Reviews

"The thirteen stories in *Mormon Underwear* capture this struggle [between Mormonism and homosexuality] with humor, sadness, insight, and sometimes shocking details....*Mormon Underwear* provides compelling stories, literally from the inside-out."

Niki D'Andrea, *Phoenix New Times*

"Townsend's lively writing style and engaging characters [in *Zombies for Jesus*] make for stories which force us to wake up, smell the (prohibited) coffee, and review our attitudes with regard to reading dogma so doggedly. These are tales which revel in the individual tics and quirks which make us human, Mormon or not, gay or not..."

A.J. Kirby, *The Short Review*

"The Rift," from *A Gay Mormon Missionary in Pompeii*, is a "fascinating tale of an untenable situation...a *tour de force*."

David Lenson, editor, *The Massachusetts Review*

"Pronouncing the Apostrophe," from *The Golem of Rabbi Loew*, is "quiet and revealing, an intriguing tale..."

Sima Rabinowitz, Literary Magazine Review, *NewPages.com*

The Circumcision of God is "a collection of short stories that consider the imperfect, silenced majority of Mormons, who may in fact be [the Church's] best hope....[The book leaves] readers regretting the church's willingness to marginalize those who best exemplify its ideals: those who love fiercely despite all obstacles, who brave challenges at great personal risk and who always choose the hard, higher road."

Kirkus Reviews

In *Mormon Fairy Tales*, Johnny Townsend displays "both a wicked sense of irony and a deep well of compassion."

Kel Munger, *Sacramento News and Review*

Zombies for Jesus is "eerie, erotic, and magical."

Publishers Weekly

"While [Townsend's] many touching vignettes draw deeply from Mormon mythology, history, spirituality and culture, [*Mormon Fairy Tales*] is neither a gaudy act of proselytism nor angry protest literature from an ex-believer. Like all good fiction, his stories are simply about the joys, the hopes and the sorrows of people."

Kirkus Reviews

"In *Inferno in the French Quarter* author Johnny Townsend restores this tragic event [the UpStairs Lounge fire] to its proper place in LGBT history and reminds us that the victims of the blaze were not just 'statistics,' but real people with real lives, families, and friends."

Jesse Monteagudo, *The Bilerico Project*

In *Inferno in the French Quarter*, "Townsend's heart-rending descriptions of the victims…seem to [make them] come alive once more."

Kit Van Cleave, *OutSmart Magazine*

Marginal Mormons is "an irreverent, honest look at life outside the mainstream Mormon Church….Throughout his musings on sin and forgiveness, Townsend beautifully demonstrates his characters' internal, perhaps irreconcilable struggles….Rather than anger and disdain, he offers an honest portrayal of people searching for meaning and community in their lives, regardless of their life choices or secrets." Named to Kirkus Reviews' Best of 2012.

Kirkus Reviews

The stories in *The Mormon Victorian Society* "register the new openness and confidence of gay life in the age of same-sex marriage….What hasn't changed is Townsend's wry, conversational prose, his subtle evocations of character and social dynamics, and his deadpan humor. His warm empathy still glows in this intimate yet clear-eyed engagement with Mormon theology and folkways. Funny, shrewd and finely wrought dissections of the awkward contradictions—and surprising harmonies—between conscience and desire." Named to Kirkus Reviews' Best of 2013.

Kirkus Reviews

"This collection of short stories [*The Mormon Victorian Society*] featuring gay Mormon characters slammed [me] in the face from the first page, wrestled my heart and mind to the floor, and left me panting and wanting more by the end. Johnny Townsend has created so many memorable characters in such few pages. I went weeks thinking about this book. It truly touched me."

Tom Webb, *A Bear on Books*

Dragons of the Book of Mormon is an "entertaining collection….Townsend's prose is sharp, clear, and easy to read, and his characters are well rendered…"

Publishers Weekly

"The pre-eminent documenter of alternative Mormon lifestyles…Townsend has a deep understanding of his characters, and his limpid prose, dry humor and well-grounded (occasionally magical) realism make their spiritual conundrums both compelling and entertaining. [*Dragons of the Book of Mormon* is] [a]nother of Townsend's critical but affectionate and absorbing tours of Mormon discontent." Named to Kirkus Reviews' Best of 2014.

Kirkus Reviews

In *Gayrabian Nights*, "Townsend's prose is always limpid and evocative, and…he finds real drama and emotional depth in the most ordinary of lives."

Kirkus Reviews

Gayrabian Nights is a "complex revelation of how seriously soul damaging the denial of the true self can be."

Ryan Rhodes, author of *Free Electricity*

Gayrabian Nights "was easily the most original book I've read all year. Funny, touching, topical, and thoroughly enjoyable."

Rainbow Awards

Lying for the Lord is "one of the most gripping books that I've picked up for quite a while. I love the author's writing style, alternately cynical, humorous, biting, scathing, poignant, and touching…. This is the third book of his that I've read, and all are equally engaging. These are stories that need to be told, and the author does it in just the right way."

Heidi Alsop, *Ex-Mormon Foundation Board Member*

In *Lying for the Lord*, Townsend "gets under the skin of his characters to reveal their complexity and conflicts....shrewd, evocative [and] wryly humorous."

Kirkus Reviews

In *Missionaries Make the Best Companions*, "the author treats the clash between religious dogma and liberal humanism with vivid realism, sly humor, and subtle feeling as his characters try to figure out their true missions in life. Another of Townsend's rich dissections of Mormon failures and uncertainties..." Named to Kirkus Reviews' Best of 2015.

Kirkus Reviews

In *Invasion of the Spirit Snatchers*, "Townsend, a confident and practiced storyteller, skewers the hypocrisies and eccentricities of his characters with precision and affection. The outlandish framing narrative is the most consistent source of shock and humor, but the stories do much to ground the reader in the world—or former world—of the characters....A funny, charming tale about a group of Mormons facing the end of the world."

Kirkus Reviews

"Townsend's collection [*The Washing of Brains*] once again displays his limpid, naturalistic prose, skillful narrative chops, and his subtle insights into psychology...Well-crafted dispatches on the clash between religion and self-fulfillment..."

Kirkus Reviews

"While the author is generally at his best when working as a satirist, there are some fine, understated touches in these tales [*The Last Days Linger*] that will likely affect readers in subtle ways....readers should come away impressed by the deep empathy he shows for all his characters—even the homophobic ones."

Kirkus Reviews

"Written in a conversational style that often uses stories and personal anecdotes to reveal larger truths, this immensely approachable book [*Racism by Proxy*] skillfully serves its intended audience of White readers grappling with complex questions regarding race, history, and identity. The author's frequent references to the Church of Jesus Christ of Latter-day Saints may be too niche for readers unfamiliar with its idiosyncrasies, but Townsend generally strikes a perfect balance of humor, introspection, and reasoned arguments that will engage even skeptical readers."

Kirkus Reviews

Orgy at the STD Clinic portrays "an all-too real scenario that Townsend skewers to wincingly accurate proportions...[with] instant classic moments courtesy of his punchy, sassy, sexy lead character..."

Jim Piechota, *Bay Area Reporter*

Orgy at the STD Clinic is "…a triumph of humane sensibility. A richly textured saga that brilliantly captures the fraying social fabric of contemporary life." Named to Kirkus Reviews' Best Indie Books of 2022.

Kirkus Reviews

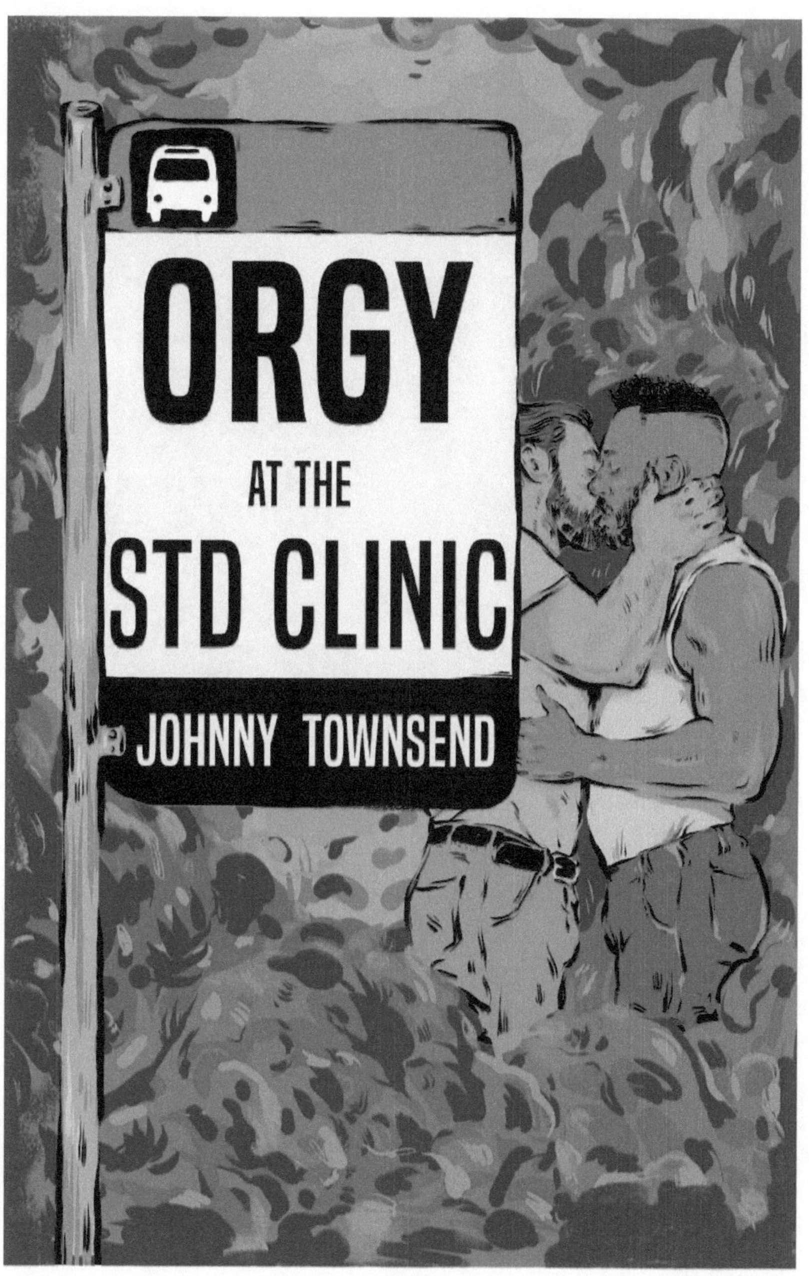

ORGY
AT THE
STD CLINIC
JOHNNY TOWNSEND

HAVE
YOUR CUM
AND
EAT IT, TOO

JOHNNY TOWNSEND

Going-Out-Of-
Religion Sale
JOHNNY TOWNSEND